THE
FORTUNATE
ISLES

Books by John Rowe Townsend

Cloudy-Bright

The Creatures

Dan Alone

Downstream

Forest of the Night

Good Night, Prof, Dear

Good-bye to the Jungle

The Intruder

The Islanders

Kate and the Revolution

Noah's Castle

Pirate's Island

The Summer People

Tom Tiddler's Ground

Top of the World

Trouble in the Jungle (*originally* Gumble's Yard)

The Visitors

Modern Poetry

A Sounding of Storytellers

Written for Children

THE FORTUNATE ISLES

A NOVEL BY

JOHN ROWE TOWNSEND

J. B. LIPPINCOTT   NEW YORK

Library of Congress Cataloging-in-Publication Data
Townsend, John Rowe.
    The Fortunate Isles / John Rowe Townsend.
        p.   cm.
    Summary: Two peasant teenagers, Eleni and Andreas, flee their native island of
Molybdos on a heroic quest, hoping to face the Living God and fulfill the ancient
prophecy that will save the Fortunate Isles from destruction.
    ISBN 0-397-32365-4 : $. — ISBN 0-397-32366-2 (lib. bdg.) : $
    [1. Adventure and adventurers—Fiction.]   I. Title.
PZ7.T6637Fp 1989   88-35690
[Fic]—dc19   CIP
                                                                         AC

To my grandchildren,
actual and potential

Author's Note

The Fortunate Isles don't now exist. Possibly they did in former times; possibly not. There are many references in myth and legend to mysterious lands—Atlantis, Avalon, Lyonesse, and others—which are either forever inaccessible or lost beneath the sea. I have supposed the Fortunate Isles to be in the Atlantic Ocean, three or four hundred miles north of Madeira. My account of them owes a good deal to Plato's Atlantis, as described in two of his *Dialogues*, and I have given their inhabitants Greek-sounding names. But I have felt free to invent as I wished. My islanders are not Greeks, and their religion and way of life are all their own.

—J.R.T.

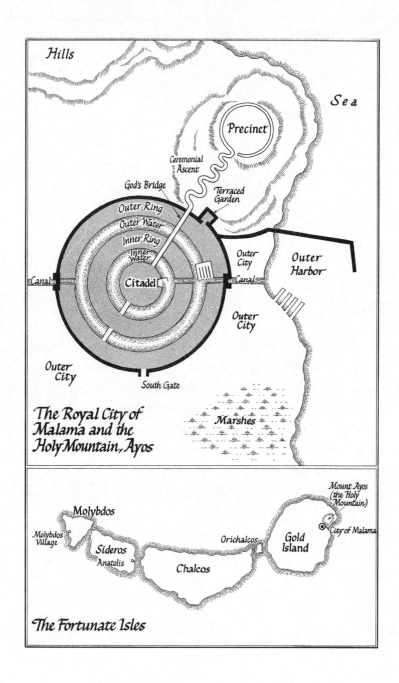

Hills

Sea

Precinct

Ceremonial
Ascent

God's Bridge

Terraced
Garden

Outer Ring

Outer Water

Inner Ring

Inner Water

Citadel

Outer
City

Outer
Harbor

Canal

Canal

Outer
City

Outer
City

South Gate

Marshes

The Royal City of
Malama and the
Holy Mountain, Ayos

Mount Ayos
(the Holy
Mountain)

Molybdos

City of Malama

Molybdos
Village

Gold
Island

Sideros

Orichalcos

Anatolis

Chalcos

The Fortunate Isles

· I ·

IN A VILLAGE OF POOR, rough children, she was the poorest and roughest. Her name was Eleni. She was scrawny and scruffy, and nobody liked her. But she had blue eyes, she met the king's son, and she set off one day on a mission to save her people.

The king's son came to Molybdos on an afternoon in spring. No one expected him. He arrived in a vessel with graceful, fluent lines and dazzling sails—a vessel that had never fished or carried cargo. It stood out at anchor in the bay, and two boats were rowed ashore. One held the king's son, the local lord, the lord's agent, and the king's son's hound. The other held half a dozen servingmen and a pile of baggage.

By the time the first boat landed, the wharf was crowded with villagers. The agent came ashore first, and waved them imperiously aside to make space. The lord—a large, pale, blond man in a spotless white cloak—came next, climbing slowly up the stone steps to stand a few paces from the agent. There was a pause. Then the king's son, holding the dog by a leather thong, ran lightly up the steps and took a position between them.

The people gazed at him in awe. They had never seen the young man before, but they knew from his appearance that he was an aristocrat. And there was something in his bearing, his air of easy confidence, the way he took the central place, that told them he was the greatest of the three, and well aware of it.

And he was beautiful. Butter-colored hair, unknown among the swarthy islanders, fell around his cheeks and was stirred by the wind. His face was lightly tanned. A brief tunic showed off his muscular but not-too-brawny limbs. He bent to pat the dog—a long, lean, nervous-looking hound—then made a smiling remark to the lord, displaying perfect teeth. He looked with lively interest at the scene around him: the villagers, the little harbor, the huddled houses that stretched up the hillside.

The headman, breathless after running from his field, pushed his way through the crowd, then halted uncertainly, not knowing whom to address. The lord's agent stepped forward.

"To your knees, Yannis!" he said. "This is the son of your king, the prince Hylas."

There were gasps from those within earshot. Yannis stared, then went awkwardly down on his knees before the young man. "Your Majesty . . ." he began.

"Royal Highness," the prince corrected him. "And get up."

Yannis, bemused, got to his feet. "Welcome, your Royal Highness," he said. "Welcome to Molybdos."

The agent said, "Prince Hylas will stay overnight in the lord's house. It is ready, Yannis, I hope?"

"Well, yes, sir, sort of. But we weren't expecting . . ."

"The lord's house should always be ready. You do not know when your lord may come, or who he may bring with him. Now tomorrow, Yannis . . ."

"Just a moment," said the prince. "I want to say a word or two."

The villagers had pressed forward, trying to hear what was being said. Hylas motioned them to stand back.

"People of this island!" he began, in a clear, ringing tone. "People of Molybdos! As the son of your king, I am delighted to be among you. I have greetings for you from the king himself, in Malama. Not only are you in his thoughts, but he has spoken of you to the Living God, and I bring you the Living God's blessing!"

There were murmurs among the people. Several of them made gestures of homage to the Living God.

"Tomorrow," Hylas continued, "I shall have an announcement to make that will delight and inspire you. And I humbly beg"—but his voice was not humble—"that every man on the island who is aged between fifteen and fifty will honor me with his presence here at noon."

"You hear, Yannis?" said the agent sharply. "That means all of them. Nobody goes out in the boats or up in the fields. And close the tavern in the morning."

3

"Sir, some of the men are at the other side of the island."

"You have plenty of time. The island is small enough. They must all be told, and all must come. You understand? It's an order."

The lord hadn't spoken so far. Now he said in a weary voice, "That deals with that, I hope. Prince Hylas and I could do with a rest and some wine."

"Certainly, my lord."

The agent led the way as the prince and the lord, with the hound still at Hylas's heels, walked through the village toward the lord's house. The men from the second boat, carrying baggage that they had unloaded, followed them to make a little procession. Neither lord nor agent looked aside, but the prince turned two or three times to smile and wave to the people.

In the lord's house, Alexis the steward and his family were busy concealing the traces of their own occupation of the lord's best rooms. Among the young people of the village there was huge excitement. Girls were in love with the prince already. Older villagers were uneasy. The people of Molybdos did not see much of its rulers. Some of the elders hinted darkly that the visit could bode no good. The lord's agent was a hard man, they said, and the lord cared nothing for their welfare. Perhaps the presence of the prince meant that some new burden was to be imposed on them. The tavern was crowded that night, and buzzing with speculation.

Eleni's older brother Milos knew of all this. He spent most of the evening in the tavern with his friends. But Eleni and her mother, Anasta, heard nothing. They had not been at the harbor to see the lord's arrival, and none of the neighbors had told them of it. Neighbors sometimes talked to Milos, but hardly ever to Anasta or Eleni.

Milos was the child of Anasta's marriage, but no one except Anasta knew who Eleni's father was. Anasta's husband had left her a year before Eleni's birth. Anasta had never lived the scandal down, and had never really tried to do so. She did not care what the village thought.

Eleni was as much apart from the village as Anasta. To begin with, there were the blue eyes, contrasting spectacularly with pitch-black hair. Nobody else on Molybdos had blue eyes. Not that they were seen as an advantage. They were a reminder of her mother's scandal, and proof that some outsider must have been involved. And in spite of her eyes Eleni was no beauty, for she had a beaky nose, a long thin face, and thick dark eyebrows. Other children called her names, and she scuffled in the dust with them, boys and girls alike, winning more fights than she lost. As she grew older, the fights became less frequent, though sometimes battles of words broke out, and in these too Eleni was generally victorious. She had a sharp and scathing tongue. But more and more the others ignored her and she ignored them.

When the king's son came to Molybdos, Eleni was fourteen, and was still straight and skinny. That evening she and her mother worked on their plot of land until dusk, then went to bed to save candles. By the time Milos came home from the tavern, they were both asleep. In the morning, very early, Eleni took the goat up to the pasture. That was when she met Hylas, who was exercising his hound.

The goat was heavy with kid. Halfway to the pasture, just where the stony track ended, Eleni heard furious barking, and the lord's dog came rushing up, excited by the presence and smell of the goat. The goat backed away, then faced the dog, horns lowered. The dog made a dart to get round the horns, but the goat was too quick and faced it again. Goat bleated, dog barked, and the noise made by the animals drowned out the shouts of approaching men. The dog made another dart and was balked again.

Eleni wasn't standing for this. With the stick she was carrying, she took a well-aimed swipe at the dog and caught it heavily on the nose. The dog fell back, demoralized and yelping. And a man came pounding up to grab it and secure it with a lead.

He was one of the prince's servingmen, although Eleni did not know it. He shouted angrily at her, speaking her own tongue but with an accent so different from hers that she could hardly understand it. His meaning was plain enough, though. He was outraged by her assault on the dog.

Eleni counterattacked. "Why don't you control the beast, you great sack of dung?" she demanded.

The man in turn understood her meaning if not all her

words, and was even more outraged. He raised his free hand as if to strike her. And at this point the king's son came up, quietly relieved him of the dog, and slipped a lead on it. The prince didn't look as radiantly handsome as he had looked on the quay, for he was wearing a thick wool garment against the morning chill, and his yellow hair was hidden under a cap such as common people wore. Eleni hardly noticed him at first, being fully occupied with the servingman. The man had grabbed her shoulders roughly with both hands and was shaking her back and forth, shouting incomprehensible threats.

"Take your filthy hands off me!" Eleni told him, and added a few remarks about his appearance and parentage. The man compared her to various female animals, indicating that the latter were cleaner and physically more attractive. At this point Hylas intervened.

"Let go of her, Dikon," he said quietly. The servingman loosed his hold. Eleni spat at him as he did so. He bristled, and once more seemed about to strike her, but the king's son stopped him with a look. In a low tone that had made courtiers tremble, the prince said to Eleni, "What do you mean by attacking my dog?"

"Didn't you see?" Eleni demanded. "He went for the goat. It's her time soon. She might have lost the kid, or worse."

"Calm down. Do you know who I am?"

"No, and I don't care," Eleni said. "I can see you're not one of *us*. I suppose you're a trader. Well, you needn't think you can pull rank on me, for all your fancy accent.

7

Most traders are crooks, if you ask me. And if you can't keep your dog under control, why don't you leave him behind where you come from?"

"He's excitable," said Hylas mildly. "And he's been too long on board ship."

"She don't know who you are, Highness," said the servingman.

"No, I can see she doesn't." Hylas took off his cap. The yellow hair fell around his cheeks. He said to Eleni, "You are looking on the son of your king."

Eleni believed him. There was truth in his manner. But she wasn't going to humble herself. "How was I to know?" she demanded. "Anyway, if somebody's dog comes worrying my goat, what do you expect me to do? Pat it on the snout?"

"Now you know who I am, you have no excuse for insolence. You're a little spitfire, aren't you? Do you know I could tell your headman to have you beaten?"

Eleni glowered. The goat, still agitated, was tugging at its cord. "I must get on and stake her out," she muttered.

Then, with sudden interest, Hylas stepped forward. "Come here, girl," he said. "Let me look at you."

Eleni raised her head defiantly. For a moment they stared at each other. Eleni said, "I know what you've seen."

"Yes. Your eyes. They're as blue as mine."

"What of it?"

"That's interesting. Very interesting. Blue eyes and black hair. I've never seen it before. What's your parentage?"

8

"It's no business of yours," Eleni said. She turned to indicate the servingman. "And it's none of *his* business, either."

"Take Whirlwind home," Hylas told the man. "I'll follow you in a few minutes. I want to talk to this girl."

The servingman looked surprised, but set off down the hill toward the lord's house. Hylas said, "Now we'll tether your goat. How far have we to go?"

"It's no distance. And I don't need any help."

"You don't refuse help from me. Come along."

Eleni trudged reluctantly beside him to the pasture and staked the goat. A neighbor, old Martha, passed them on the way and stared. Eleni stared her down.

"Now," Hylas said, "I want to know about you. What is your name?"

"Eleni."

"You are not beautiful, Eleni."

"You don't need to tell me that. I know it."

"Or even attractive."

"I know that, too. So why follow me around?"

"Eleni, are your parents living?"

"My mother's alive. My father may be dead for all I know. My mother hasn't told me or anyone else. I don't know who he is or was. It doesn't make any difference to me."

"Eleni, those eyes. Do you not know that in these islands blue eyes are noble? All aristocrats are blue-eyed. But they are also fair-haired. I've never before seen blue eyes with raven-black hair like yours. It's quite striking."

Eleni was unimpressed.

"It's never done *me* any good," she said. "Maybe one of your lords came around here one time, doing what he shouldn't. That's what they say in the village. I can tell you, I'm not thankful for the color of my eyes. If eyes could be dyed, I'd dye them. And now, have you finished? I have work to do."

"Yes, I've finished. But you interest me, Eleni. I've never in my life heard so much impudence from a common person. I wonder if you can really be a common person. Have you ever left this island?"

"No."

"Perhaps someday you will. Perhaps you'll come to Gold Island: to Malama, the golden city. Remember me, Eleni. We may meet again if I don't get killed; who knows? And, Eleni, in the Fortunate Isles all nobles call one another 'cousin.' Perhaps you have noble blood and I should call you 'cousin.' How would you like that?"

"I wouldn't," said Eleni, and went.

After she'd gone a few steps, the prince called her name. She looked around and saw a small, glittering object fly through the air toward her. It looked like a coin. She ignored it and went on her way; but she'd noted where it fell, and when the prince had gone, she went back and found it. She took it home and told her mother of the encounter.

"It's gold," Anasta said. "A ten-helion piece. It's as much as your brother Milos earns in a year."

Eleni's eyes widened.

"What shall we do with it?" she asked.

"We'll put it by and say nothing. If Milos gets to know about it, it'll all be spent in the tavern."

Anasta went to a corner of the wall, felt with her fingers, and found a tiny opening into which she tucked the coin.

"That's where it is," she said. "If ever you need it, it's yours."

"He asked me who my father was," Eleni said. "I told him I didn't know. Maybe it's time you told me."

"Well, I'm not going to!" Anasta snapped. "Not now or any other time! So you needn't ask me again!" Then, softening her tone, she added, "You did right not to encourage that young man, even if he *is* a prince. I don't want you having any dealings with the nobility. No good can come of it."

Eleni knew from long experience that it was no use arguing with her mother. She said no more. But Hylas had made a deep impression on her. His appearance, his manner, his voice were so different from those of anyone on Molybdos. She'd been careful not to seem overawed by him on the spot, but an encounter with the king's son was far and away the most interesting thing that had ever happened to her. She wasn't likely to forget that he'd said they might meet again.

It was Milos who broke the news to Anasta and Eleni. He burst into the cottage as they were finishing their midday meal and shouted, "I'm going to be a soldier!"

"You're *what*?" Anasta demanded.

"I'm going to a war. I was first to enlist! All the lads are joining!"

"Are you crazy?"

"It's Prince Hylas, isn't it?" said Eleni slowly.

"You've heard about him, then. Yes, of course it's Prince Hylas. He called all the men to the wharf and spoke to us. What a speech! You should have heard it! He was tremendous! You can tell he's a leader, just by looking and listening to him. Inspiring—that's the word. By the time he'd finished, I'd have followed him anywhere!"

"But what's the war about?" Anasta asked.

"It's us against the mainland. I don't know why, exactly. What's it matter? It's a war, and we're going to win it. We'll be well paid. Free food, free battle gear, money, and loot as well, when we've won."

"And what if we don't win?"

"Oh, we're bound to, under Hylas. He leads from in front, not behind. And we have the Living God on our side. Hylas told us so, and so did the priest."

"I wouldn't put much faith in the Living God," said Anasta. "The Living God never did anything for me, or anyone I know of."

"Well, he wouldn't for the likes of us, would he? It's the priests and nobles he listens to. You ought to know that."

"I don't want you to go," said Anasta.

"You can't stop me, Mother," said Milos. "And don't you realize, this is the greatest chance we've ever had? What is there for young people on Molybdos? Hard work

12

and poverty and boredom, that's what there is, and I want to get away from it. And so do all the others!"

"Do you have any choice?"

"Oh, yes. Hylas only wants volunteers."

"Don't go, then. It never makes sense to do something you don't have to do—not if you're poor. It isn't the poor that benefit. Besides, what will I do without the bit you give me from your wages?"

"We won't be away for long, Hylas says. Back home for harvest. And we'll come back rich. He promised us that. The wages I earn are nothing anyway."

"They're something to me and Eleni. Anyway, I want my son alive, not dead."

"It's no good fussing, Mother. I've made up my mind. It's the chance of a lifetime, and I'm taking it. There's a ship on the way from Gold Island, picking up men. And when it sails, I'll be on board!"

· II ·

PRINCE HYLAS SAILED the same day, in the beautiful ship that had brought him to Molybdos. With him went the local lord, who lived on the next island in the chain that made up the Fortunate Isles. Molybdos was the end of the chain, and was Hylas's last port of call in the recruiting drive. It was another three days before a big, heavy merchant ship arrived from Gold Island to pick up the men who'd enlisted.

The volunteers went aboard at once, having first been blessed on the quayside by the priest, Mikele, in the name of the Living God. The villagers expected the ship to sail soon afterward, but in fact it remained at anchor in the bay for another two days. The men who had gone on board were not seen again, but two tough, grizzled officers, with a squad of equally tough, brawny soldiers, came ashore to look for more recruits.

Enlistment, it turned out, was not as voluntary as the prince had made it seem. The recruiting squad visited every house in the village, and then the outlying farms. Men who had not volunteered were first invited to do so, then heavily persuaded. Some who saw the process said it was more like compulsion than persuasion. The later men to enlist got no blessing from Mikele, who had sobered up enough to bless the first volunteers but was now drunk again. His attendant, Andreas, the headman's sixteen-year-old son, could not give blessings.

On the second day recruiting in the village was completed, and the squad spread out to investigate the farms and the tiny fishing hamlet at the other side of the island. There was sullen resistance by now, and some of the men went into hiding, but few escaped the net. The lord's steward, Alexis, was suspected of acting as an informer, though he denied it. In the end barely a dozen of the young and middle-aged men remained, and most of these were unfit. Among those who contrived to stay behind was the steward's son Nikos, aged eighteen.

Whether Prince Hylas knew what was going on or was himself a victim of deception it was impossible to say. By the time the merchant ship sailed, many islanders were cursing him. Anasta was among the most bitter. Eleni agreed with what Anasta had to say, and feared for Milos's life, though she and her half-brother had not got on well. Yet she could not put from her mind the butter-yellow hair and the dizzying suggestion from the king's son that he should call her "cousin."

———

Two or three days after the men's departure, the head-man, Yannis, called at Anasta's cottage. It was evening. She and Eleni were both at home. Anasta let him in without enthusiasm; Yannis had seldom taken notice of her before.

Seeing her frown, Yannis grinned apologetically.

"Well, Anasta," he said, "I never thought I'd come here seeking you out, after all these years. But things are different from what they were a few days ago. We're all in the same boat now."

Anasta gave him a hostile look. "I can't see that you and me's in the same boat," she said. "*Your* son's safe, being the Living God's priest's assistant and not fit for fighting. I don't know where *my* son is or what will become of him. What's the same about that?"

"Now, now, Anasta. There's no need for that tone of voice. I see you haven't changed your nature. You always had a sharp tongue. You've changed on the outside, of course. We none of us get any younger." He turned to Eleni. "You might be surprised, young woman, if you could see your mother as she used to be. She was a good looker, I can tell you. We all admired her, until . . ." His voice trailed away.

"Until I disgraced myself?" Anasta said. "You haven't come here to go through all *that* again, have you?"

"No, no, that's not it," Yannis said. "I've something to tell you as headman. You know that until the lads come back, we're short of able-bodied men."

"Well?"

"Well, there's work that has to be done. If the men aren't here to do it, the girls and women must."

"There's no point in telling *me* that. Eleni and I are working all we have strength for already. It takes the two of us to keep our bit of land going."

"What I'm telling you," said Yannis, "is that Eleni will be needed for the fishing."

Anasta faced him, furious.

"Nothing doing!" she said. "I've lost Milos. I need Eleni. Anyway, you know women don't go in the boats. The men say it's unlucky to have a woman in a boat. They won't change their minds now."

"Eleni's not what you could call a woman," Yannis said.

"Of course she's a woman. She'll be fifteen soon."

"Well, she don't *look* like a woman. A woman is . . ." Yannis drew a curve with his hand. "Now Eleni's as thin as a lad, and she wears what a lad would wear. Nobody would know she's a girl, unless they was told. And at a time like this we've no choice. I can't make up a crew for my second boat without her."

"I don't mind going fishing," said Eleni.

"You be quiet!" Anasta told her sharply. Then, to Yannis, "There's all sorts of problems with having a young girl on the boats. I don't have to tell you. And ocean fishing's dangerous. She might get drowned."

"That's a risk we all take. Do you think I don't know about it? Three boats lost in the last ten years. Twelve lives, and one of them my own brother's. We can't afford to lose any more now. If it's any comfort to you, I'm sending my own lad on the *Seahawk*, along with Eleni. And I'm sending Nikos as well."

Eleni made a face at the mention of Nikos. He was bossy and arrogant, and made the most of being the steward's son. She would not have chosen him as a companion. But she said nothing. Her heart had leaped at the thought of going fishing. Since she'd been a small child, she had envied the boys who would grow up to man the boats. That was a better life than scratching at the soil, and she would seize any chance of it, even if it meant being with Nikos.

As for Yannis's son Andreas . . . Anasta was asking about him already. "You mean Andreas isn't going to help the priest anymore?" she asked.

"No. Mikele will have to do without a helper."

"How will the drunken sot manage?"

"That's his problem," said Yannis. "Mikele'll have to pull himself together. Fact is, I need all hands, and that includes Andreas. So you see, Anasta, you and me *is* in the same boat. My lad and your girl: If we lost one of them we'd most likely lose them both. It's equal chances. But the Living God grant we don't lose either. As for Milos, let's hope it's over as soon as they say. Keep cheerful, Anasta. I daresay the lads'll come home covered with glory and laden with loot. You won't be envying me then. When that day arrives, you'll be *proud* of Milos."

"*If* that day arrives!" said Anasta grimly. "I'll tell you

18

straight what I think about all that war-making, Yannis. You mark my words. No good will come of it, none at all!"

Yannis was the headman, and got his way. Two days later Eleni was a member of the crew of the *Seahawk*, trawling for hake and monkfish and anything edible that the waters around Molybdos might yield. The *Seahawk* was a stumpy, cumbersome vessel, safe and seaworthy but hard to sail against the wind. Klito, who skippered her, was a man of over seventy, vastly experienced but failing in strength. Petros, who supplied the brawn of the crew, was large, lumbering, and slow. The recruiting officers had turned him down as hopelessly stupid.

Nikos, in his own opinion, supplied the brains, and was usually at the helm. Andreas and Eleni did the menial jobs. They put out and drew in the nets, unloaded the boat when she returned to harbor, sorted the catch, and swabbed the decks. Andreas had been a weakling as a child, and although he was now quite healthy, he was still not physically strong. He was treated with scorn by all.

It was a hard life. Eleni had expected that and didn't mind it. But she was soon dissatisfied. She had sailed small boats, as had all the village children, and she wanted to take the helm of the *Seahawk*. Nikos wouldn't yield it to her, even for a moment, and ordered her around unmercifully. When she argued with him, he hit her.

"She wants to be treated like a lad," he told Klito on one occasion, "so I'm treating her like a lad. That's what I'd do to a lad of her age who tried telling *me* what to do."

19

And he clouted her again. Twice Eleni went for him like a wildcat and was soundly beaten. Once, in harbor, Eleni took Nikos by surprise; he lost his footing under her assault and fell full-length in the squirming, wetly flapping catch. He struggled furiously to his feet, seized a kicking, biting Eleni, and tried to push her overboard. Petros, who usually stayed neutral, stepped in and held them apart until they calmed down.

Then the day came when, in blustery wind, Nikos was hit by the boom and dislocated his shoulder. He was out of action and in agony. Klito hadn't the strength to take the helm in rough conditions, and Petros was needed to wield the heavy oar and bring the boat around at the end of each tack. Eleni had to be helmsman. She hung grimly to the sheet, though flung to and fro and at times almost hurled into the air. The *Seahawk* came safely into harbor. Andreas took Nikos to the priest's house and gave him a draft to dull the pain. Then, with difficulty, Andreas woke the priest, who was just sober enough to put the shoulder back.

From then on Eleni was treated with more respect. She was sometimes allowed to take the helm, and rapidly became skilled. Both Klito and Nikos admitted that she was a quick learner, though Klito was never quite convinced that a woman's presence wouldn't bring his boat to grief. Eleni grew tougher than ever, lean and muscular; she learned to read the night sky, to know the reefs and currents, to find the most promising fishing grounds. In the scant time when she was not at sea, maintaining the boat and nets, or asleep, she helped Anasta to till the plot of land.

As the weeks went by, a friendship grew between Eleni and Andreas. At the age of twelve, Andreas had become attendant and server to Mikele, the priest, who (like all priests in the Fortunate Isles) was also the healer. Mikele was drunken and lazy, but meant well, and in his periods of sobriety had taught Andreas to read. Andreas had also learned a little about medicines and the care of wounds, but he hadn't yet been initiated into such mysteries as reading omens, predicting the future, and interpreting the will of the Living God.

"Would you believe it," Andreas said to Eleni one day, "old Mikele has stacks of writings in his house. Roll upon roll of writing. We found it a year ago in the cave where the priests used to live in the old days. Mikele's read a bit of it, but there's a lot that he hasn't even looked at; he's too lazy. And he won't let *me* read it, in case there's stuff that only priests should know."

Andreas sighed. "I wish the men would come back," he said. "Then I could get on with my serving years. I still have so much to learn before I can be a priest myself. And Mikele will retire in a year or two, if he hasn't drunk himself to death by then. I'd like to take over from him."

Eleni made a face. "I don't think I want you to be priest," she said.

"I'd be a better priest than Mikele, though I must say he's not so bad at the healing, when he's sober. I'd like to learn more about that."

"I wouldn't mind learning something about healing myself," said Eleni. "More use than the Living God stuff, if you ask me."

"I don't know if a girl would be allowed to learn," said Andreas. "Anyway, what chance has either of us of learning anything when we're stuck in this stinking old tub, hauling nets in or swabbing decks?"

Eleni didn't feel the same way as Andreas about fishing. She loved to be out on the ocean; she loved the changing waters and the changing skies, and sometimes she felt the sea sang in her veins. She loved to be active and to be at the helm. She loved anything that fed her sense of adventure. While she longed for the men to return, and knew how much Molybdos needed them, she feared she would lose her place in the boat when they came back.

In any case, that was not what happened. One day in late summer the merchantman that had taken the men away came back into the bay. A single boat brought ashore those who were returning to Molybdos. There were only eight of them, and all were sick or wounded. From Molybdos they had been shipped to Gold Island, to fight in a war of conquest against a mainland kingdom. The first and only battle had brought crushing defeat. Many of the fighting ships had been rammed and sunk, and the men aboard them had been either drowned or sold into slavery. Of the Molybdos men who escaped these hazards, the able-bodied ones had been held on Gold Island by the king to await the next assault on the mainland or sent to Orichalcos to work in the royal mines.

Among the eight who returned was Eleni's brother, Milos. His left foot had been wounded, then crudely amputated. After examining the stump, Mikele declared that it was healing well and Milos could thank the Living God that he had been miraculously spared death from gangrene. But Milos, thin and drawn and looking much older, was not disposed to be thankful. His bitterness was even greater than Anasta's.

It was some time before Eleni brought herself to ask him if anything had been seen of Prince Hylas.

"Oh, he was there all right," Milos said, "exhorting the troops, and leading us into battle. I must admit, he went into the thick of things. And much good it did!"

"Was he killed?"

"No, he was captured."

"And was *he* sold into slavery?"

"Not on your life. He was ransomed. He's back on Gold Island now. I wonder if he's changed his mind about going to war the way *we* have."

There was a cynical look on Milos's face. "War's all right for *some*," he said.

·III·

AT THE END OF SUMMER, when the corn was almost ripe for cutting, storms came. There had never been such storms in living memory. The wheat and barley were soaked and flattened. Torrential rain washed the soil from hillside vegetable plots. Day after day the fishing boats stayed in the little harbor, imprisoned by dangerous seas. From time to time there was a brief respite; then the storms came back, more fierce, it seemed, than ever.

After three weeks calm returned and the sun shone; but by then Molybdos faced disaster. People were hungry, and likely to remain so throughout the winter. Nothing was plentiful except wine; and that was of less than no use, for the few men who were around sat hour by hour in the tavern, drowning their woes and dulling their wits. Yannis thought of closing the tavern, but decided realistically that he couldn't get away with it. He sent Kostas, a wounded soldier, to the lord's agent on neighboring Sideros to ask for help, but Kostas came back with the reply that Sideros too had been hit by storms and had lost men in the war. Sideros had nothing to spare.

Mikele, the priest, appealed to the Living God, with appropriate ritual but no result. The god, he said, must be angry with Molybdos; but Mikele didn't know what the offense had been. He suggested, hopefully, that offerings brought to him might turn away divine wrath. But the villagers had little to offer, and though they had faith in the Living God, they knew Mikele too well to believe the god would take much notice of him; Mikele, like the rest, felt the pinch of hard times.

"Mikele keeps muttering about some kind of rescue," Andreas told Eleni. "Says things are so bad the 'time must come,' whatever that means. I think he knows something the others don't. You should come with me and see him sometime. He's lonely and needs a bit of company. And we could ask him if he'll teach you some healing."

Eleni didn't see much hope at present of having leisure to learn anything. Her life was hard. Anasta expected a lot of work from her, tired though she was from the fishing. Her brother, Milos, was bitter, unhelpful, and often in pain from his wound. But Andreas was anxious to take her to see Mikele, and on a morning when the tide prevented the *Seahawk* from putting early to sea, they set off together for the priest's house.

The house was at the top of the hill behind the village,

close to the Living God's shrine and to the cave where Mikele's predecessors had lived. The orders of worship laid down that every shrine in the Fortunate Isles must be in sight of Mount Ayos, the Holy Mountain, on Gold Island. On a clear day the top of the mountain could just be seen, fifty miles away to the east. Up there, as everyone knew, was the domain of the Living God.

Eleni and Andreas climbed to the priest's house together. It was a bright, sharp day, and in morning light the mountain seemed to float, frail and miragelike, on the horizon. Andreas was delighted. "A day we can see the mountain's an auspicious day," he told Eleni. "When you look at it, doesn't it give you a kind of tingle? A feeling that the god is *there?*"

"Can't say I've felt it."

Andreas smiled. "One day you will," he said.

As they approached the priest's house, Mikele lurched out, shirtless. He was a large, potbellied old man with a wild tangle of hair. He made his way to the pump and held his head under the spout. Then, gasping and spluttering and not having seen his visitors, he shook his gray mane, straightened up, and went back into the house. Andreas went in after him, and beckoned from the doorway for Eleni to follow. She did so reluctantly.

The priest's house was filthy. Its one living room smelled of unwashed clothes and bedding, of ancient garbage, and of wine and urine. Wine jars lay around everywhere. Mikele dragged on a ragged shirt, then slumped onto a broken-down couch.

26

"High time you showed your face!" he growled to Andreas. "You don't come often, now you're on the fishing. Haven't seen you in a long time!"

"I was here two days ago," Andreas said. "You've forgotten."

"I don't forget things. And where's your manners? What do you call me, eh?"

"Master."

"That's better. Two days, you say? Well, two days *is* a long time. Where were you yesterday?"

"Out in the boat."

"Have you brought me a fish for my dinner?"

"No. We didn't catch much, and they were watching me all the time when we got to the wharf."

"I might have guessed. When's that Yannis going to let you come back to me? That's what I want to know."

"He still says he can't spare me."

"Much use *you* are in a boat, I'll wager!"

Andreas reddened and said nothing. Mikele leaned from the couch, poured himself a cup of wine, downed it at a gulp, and poured another. He gave Andreas a sly, sideways look.

"I know what you're thinking," he said. "I drink too much, too early. But let me tell you, it's hard, being single and not as young as you were. Now your father's a sober man, but it's all very well for him. He has a wife to look after him. I have only myself. Wine is my father and mother, my wife and children. I can't do without it."

His eye fell on Eleni.

———

"Who's that lad lingering in the doorway?" he demanded. "What right have you to bring folk here without asking. What right, eh? You, boy, come inside and step over here. Let's have a look at you."

"She's not a boy . . ." Andreas began. But Mikele didn't hear him. He was gazing into the face of Eleni as she moved toward him. With an effort he got up from the couch, stepped forward in turn, gripped Eleni by the shoulders, and stared at her. Eleni stared hard back.

"It's him!" said the priest. "Or else I'm mad. It's him!"

"It's not a him," said Andreas. "It's a her."

Again Mikele seemed not to hear him. "By the god himself!" he said. "It's the Messenger. I believe he's the Messenger!"

Eleni wriggled her shoulders from the priest's grip and stepped back. At close range she was repelled by the priest's red-rimmed eyes, by the broken veins in his nose and cheeks, and above all by his breath, at once foul and wine-laden. In a loud, clear voice she said, "I am not a lad. I'm Anasta's Eleni. Anasta's the woman who never goes to worship. And I don't go to worship either. That's why you don't know me. But Anasta's Eleni's who I am."

Mikele said slowly, "Why are you here?"

"Andreas brought me." Although she'd pulled herself free, Eleni still seemed to feel the priest's heavy hands on her shoulders, and to smell the horrible breath. Looking at the wild gray hair and watery eyes, she shuddered. She didn't want to have any kind of contact with this man. "And I wish he hadn't," she added.

Mikele turned to Andreas. "He *has* to be a lad. He *must* be. His voice'll break soon. Won't it?"

"I don't know what you mean, Master. This is Anasta's Eleni. I thought you might let her learn a bit about the healing."

Mikele sank back onto the couch, groped around for his empty cup, and refilled it. He still seemed only half convinced.

"You're *sure* she's a girl?" he asked Andreas. "*How* are you sure?"

Andreas blushed a second time. "I've known Eleni since she was little," he said. "Of course she's a girl."

"Oh, come on!" said Eleni crossly. "I've had enough of this. He'll be wanting to see for himself in a minute!"

Andreas, still crimson-faced but dogged, said, "Just a moment, Eleni. I *have* to ask him something. Master, you talked about a Messenger. What did you mean?"

Mikele's expression became crafty. "I didn't mean anything," he said. "It was a mistake."

"It sounded important," Andreas said.

"It's nothing to do with you. I'm tired of you this morning, boy. I don't know why I wanted you back. Maybe when all this is over I'll ask your father to give me someone else. You're too inquisitive by half. Get out of here and mind your own business!"

Andreas stood his ground, though Eleni could see that he was nervous. He said, "Master, you *must* tell me. When you thought Eleni was a boy, you said this must be the Messenger. Why?"

"I said mind your own business."

Andreas said, "Things are bad on the island. We're close to starving. If you know something that would help us, Master, you mustn't keep it dark. Surely the god wouldn't want you to."

"Don't you start telling *me* what the god wants!" the priest said. He was silent for a moment. Then he went on, in a different tone of voice, "Sorry, lad. I shouldn't have shouted at you. You're a good boy. And the truth is, I don't know these days *what* the god wants. I seem to have lost touch with him. I do the right things, but nothing happens. The sooner you're trained and ready to take over, the better. As for what I said just now, well, the cat's halfway out of the bag already, and maybe I should tell you. And the girl can stay, because she's the cause of it."

Mikele's hand went out, as if automatically, for the cup.

"You know," he went on, "there've been a lot of priests here on Molybdos. Forty or fifty, they say, perhaps more. Nobody knows exactly. We follow on, one after another. Some of us aren't too clever, and some of us have our little weaknesses"—he glanced at the cup in his hand—"but I suppose we've all done our best according to our lights. We try to find out what the Living God wants, by the methods that were taught to us, and sometimes we can and sometimes we can't. And often we're not sure. But none of us have *seen* the god. Except Themis."

"Tell Eleni who Themis was," said Andreas.

"He was the priest here hundreds of years ago—the most famous priest we ever had. He was a very holy man, and had visions. One day, when the Holy Mountain was clearer than it had ever been before, when Themis had fasted and prayed, he saw the Living God, and the god entered into him, and he prophesied to the people of Molybdos. He left an account of it. It's in one of those scrolls that were found in the cave."

"Have you read it?" Andreas asked.

"Well, not exactly. It's a bit faded, and all in funny old words. Tell you the truth, I tried and I couldn't make much of it. Maybe you'll do better one of these days. But I don't have to read it to know what it says. We hand a lot of things down by word of mouth, from one priest to the next. You think I'm ignorant, young Andreas, but I may know more than you think."

"So what did Themis prophesy?"

"He said there would come a time when the people of Molybdos were oppressed and starving. And when that time came, a Messenger would be found who would save them. The priest would recognize the Messenger when he arrived, and could proclaim him to the people, but until then he was to hold his peace and not make the prophecy known. So maybe I've said more than I should have in telling you."

"*How* was the priest to recognize the Messenger?" Andreas asked.

"*I* know," said Eleni. "The eyes."

"That's right. The priest would know the Messenger, Themis said, by his black hair and blue eyes."

"And what's the Messenger supposed to do?"

"He must make his way, defeating all threats and overcoming all obstacles, to Gold Island, and thence to the Holy Mountain. Once there he must climb to the summit and find the Living God."

There was a stunned silence. Andreas said, "It's impossible. There isn't a man or boy on Molybdos with the right color eyes and hair, and even if there were, my father wouldn't let him go. He believes in the god, of course, but he'd say it was a wild-goose chase. I can just hear him saying it."

"When the Messenger's found the Living God," said Eleni, "what's the Living God going to do about it?"

"That we're not told," said Mikele. "The Living God does as he thinks fit. There's no point in mortal folk like us trying to guess how the Living God will act. We'd have to be gods ourselves, to understand the mind of the god."

Eleni said, "I don't believe in it. But I wish I was this Messenger, all the same. If only I could have a go at that! I mean, compared with that, digging the garden and even fishing aren't worth a fig. I'd be on my way like an arrow from a bow! Oh, why does it have to be a lad?"

Andreas had been deep in thought. Now he said, "Master. Did Themis actually *say* the Messenger must be a man?"

"He said the Messenger must be young, that's all I know. But that means a young man. Of course it does. It stands to reason."

Andreas said, "You *thought* Eleni was a boy. And Eleni goes out in the boats, just like one of the men. If she can be a fisherman, she can be a messenger, can't she? Master, you were right in the first place. She *is* the one. She *has* to be the one!"

"It wouldn't do," Mikele said faintly. "There's never been anything like it."

"There's never been anything like the state we're in on Molybdos just now."

"Have some sense, Andreas. How could a young girl go off alone on a journey like that?"

"Does the Messenger *have* to go alone?" Andreas asked.

"I never heard that anyone was to go with him. Though, for that matter, I never heard that they shouldn't. There's a lot more on the scroll than I've told you. But, like I say, I haven't read it myself. And this is silly talk. You think I'm going to proclaim this young lass as the Messenger? I'd be a laughingstock!"

Eleni had stopped listening. Excitement was rising in her.

"It's me!" she cried. "It's me! I'm off to Gold Island! I'll climb the Holy Mountain!"

"You're out of your mind, girl!" said Mikele roughly. "You're not going anywhere, except where you're told. Yannis won't have you tearing away on mad errands, nor would your mother. You can forget all about this. By the sacred name, I wish I hadn't told you. Down to the harbor, now, both of you, and get on with your fishing!"

The priest reached out for the wine jar and poured the last of its contents into his cup. His hands were trembling.

"It's no good arguing with him," Andreas told Eleni. "I know when Mikele's made up his mind." They left.

Outside, the day was still clear, and the mountain hung—faint, transparent, magical-looking—in the distant air. Andreas said, "I believe in that prophecy. And I believe it could be you. But you always say you don't believe in religion at all."

"Oh, I can believe in *that!*" declared Eleni. And suddenly, gazing at the mountain, she did believe. She was the Messenger and she could do anything. Of *course* she could go to Gold Island. Of *course* she could climb the mountain and find the Living God. Of *course* the god existed. She wasn't sure he hadn't just spoken to her, this very minute. Certainly something amazing had happened in her mind, something to change her world. . . .

And there was another thing. Prince Hylas was on Gold Island and had said he might see her if she ever went there. If she was the Messenger and could find the Living God, surely she could find a prince as well.

There was a wild gleam in her eye. "I'm going," she said, "and they can't stop me."

"Mikele was right," said Andreas. "You *are* crazy. But *I'm* not crazy, and if you're going on a mad quest, I'm going with you. You realize, Eleni, my dad won't give permission for either of us to go. But if we came back successful, he'd be proud of me at last. As for your mother . . ."

"She wouldn't let me go, either. So I shan't tell her."

"Can she manage without you, Eleni?"

"Well, it'll be hard. She'll miss me. But she can get by, just about. And maybe when I've gone Milos'll turn his hand to helping her. There's a lot he can do, in spite of his foot, if he has a mind to."

"We'll have to sneak away," Andreas said. "That will take planning."

"All right, we'll plan it, then," said Eleni. "Or you can." Her expression was faraway, and her mind was on more heroic things than planning.

Andreas smiled. "And may the Living God protect us!" he said.

·IV·

IN THE NEXT THREE DAYS of hard work and long hours, Eleni had no time or opportunity to work out with Andreas how they could escape from Molybdos and make their way to Gold Island. But the determination to do so didn't fade. Going to sleep and waking up, she had visions of journeying over unknown landscapes, of distant hills and valleys, of woods and rivers and seacoasts and villages, and at last the rumored splendors of Malama and the unknown mysteries of the Holy Mountain. Her brief moment of belief in the Living God had not lasted, but the belief in herself and the hope of adventure had remained. She was as sure as ever that there would be some marvelous outcome to her quest. And into all her imaginings came the figure of Hylas, his beauty enhanced in her memory.

Andreas was shouted at by Nikos several times for being slow or not listening to orders. Eleni, who was equally inattentive, didn't get shouted at. This was because Nikos was becoming aware of her femininity. Twice she felt his arm go around her waist, and once he whispered in her ear, suggesting that she meet him after work for a bit of fun. She slapped his face for that, but Nikos merely laughed. At other times Nikos infuriated her by breaking loudly into song, for he was boastfully proud of his singing voice. She would be glad to get away from him.

On the fourth day, with tide and wind unfavorable and a wretched catch, the *Seahawk* returned early to harbor. Klito, Petros, and Nikos disappeared into the tavern, leaving Eleni and Andreas to clear up. This gave them, at last, a chance to talk together.

"Well . . . ?" inquired Eleni.

Andreas looked back at her and nodded. "I still want to go," he said.

"Do you think they'll come after us?"

"They might. Depends how soon they realize what we're doing."

"They're bound to miss us," Eleni said. "And Mikele will tell them."

"Mikele won't. I saw him before I came down to the quay this morning. Mikele's worried, Eleni. I reckon we half convinced him. He's not going to proclaim you the Messenger, because as he says he'd make a fool of himself. But if you *were* the Messenger and he stopped you, he reckons he'd be in trouble with the Living God. I mean, just imagine it—a priest missing a call like that!"

"So what's he going to do about it?"

"Nothing. They're bound to ask him what he knows, of course, seeing I was his helper. But he'll just say he doesn't know anything. So far as he's concerned, we never said a word. So if we get ourselves killed or come back in disgrace or whatever, he won't lose face. And if we succeed, *then* he'll say he knew all along and it was all his idea. So he'll get the credit."

"The cunning old so-and-so!" said Eleni, half shocked and half admiring. Then, "Does it mean we'll get any help from him?"

"I got a bit of advice, that's all."

"It's easy to give advice. What did he say?"

"He told me which way we should go. The important thing, he says, is to steer clear of Orichalcos, where they grab you and put you to work in the orichalc mines. Wherever we go, we must try not to draw attention to ourselves. And we must take money."

"Money!" Eleni was dismayed. The people of Molybdos didn't make much use of money. Mostly they lived on what they produced, with the help of a good deal of swapping.

"Alexis has money," Andreas said, "being the lord's steward. And Dinos at the tavern; he gets it from visiting sailors. Anybody who deals with folk from other islands needs money. Well, *our* first step is to get off *this* island. We have to cross the straits to Sideros. Mikele says old

Tonios at the ferry charges two selenicas each for the crossing, and if we wanted him to forget he'd seen us, he'd charge another two each. That's eight selenicas."

"Eight selenicas! I haven't even *one* selenica. We'll have to find another way."

"Even if we could, we'd still need money to buy food. We can't take enough food with us for a journey like that."

Then, as Andreas was speaking, Eleni remembered the gold coin thrown to her by Hylas. It had been given to her, and Anasta had said it was hers if she needed it.

"Come along with me," she said. She led Andreas around the hillside to Anasta's cottage. Anasta was out in the field. "Keep out of sight."

Eleni crept into the house, felt for the hole in the wall, and briefly panicked when she found the wrong place and thought the coin was gone. But a moment later her fingers closed on it. She swiftly slipped away again, unseen, and showed the coin in triumph to Andreas.

"Ten helions!" he said. "That's a lot of money. It's a hundred selenicas. Enough to buy food for us all the way to Malama. But there's a snag, Eleni."

"What's that?"

"It's too much money all tied up in one coin. Ordinary people don't have that kind of money. It'd be no good trying to buy bread or milk at a farm with a coin like this; they wouldn't have change. It's more money than they've ever had at one time."

"So what can we do?"

"There's only one person on Molybdos who would have money on that scale. That's Nikos's dad, Alexis. He's been the lord's steward for twenty years, and he's always on the make. We'll have to get *him* to change it."

"He'll cheat us!" said Eleni.

"I expect he will. But what can we do? We can't tell anybody what we're up to. We'd better go and see Alexis now."

The lord's house stood a little above the village and over-looked the harbor. It was by far the biggest and most handsome house on Molybdos. Neither the lord nor his agent had been seen on the island since Prince Hylas's visit, and the steward had settled back into his usual way of life, treating house and servants as if they were his own. He was a polite, smiling man, and nobody trusted him an inch. "He'd smile at you to your face and stab you in the back," the villagers said of him, and "He'd sell his grand-mother for a selenica."

It was Nikos, back from the tavern and slightly flushed, who opened the door of the lord's house. He stared at Eleni and Andreas. "What do *you* want?" he demanded.

"We want to see your father," Eleni said.

"What about?"

"That's our business. Just tell him we're here, will you?" Andreas said.

"Not unless you tell me what you want."

But at this point Alexis himself appeared. "What's all this about?" he inquired. "These young people wish to see me? Well, that's all right. Here I am. I always believe in making myself available. Come into my business room."

Nikos retired, disgruntled. In the business room Alexis inquired courteously after Andreas's father and Eleni's mother. "A remarkable woman, Anasta," he said. "A pity she keeps herself so much to herself. Though perhaps not surprising. . . ."

Eleni scowled. Andreas said hastily, "Show him the coin, Eleni."

Alexis took the coin from Eleni's hand, blinked at it in surprise, and bit it. Then he asked, suspiciously, "Where did you get this?"

"It was given to me," Eleni said.

"Who by?"

"A visitor. From Gold Island."

"*What* visitor?"

"I can't tell you."

"And what do you want me to do with it?"

"Change it for selenicas," said Andreas.

Alexis was silent for a while, turning the coin over and over in his hand. Then he asked Eleni, "Did your mother send you?"

"No."

"She doesn't know about this?"

"No."

Alexis demanded sharply, "Did you steal it from her?"

"No, I did not!"

"I can understand that Anasta might have it," the steward said, half to himself, half to Eleni. "It could have something to do with your birth. I've always known there was more to that than ever came out. Somebody paid for his pleasure, perhaps. . . ."

Eleni, outraged, was within an inch of slapping the steward's face. He was not disturbed by her fury, but smiled again.

"Well, young woman," he said, "suppose I accept your tale that you came by this honestly, and I change it for you. In confidence, of course. What would you expect to get for it?"

Andreas said, "It's worth a hundred selenicas."

"It's not worth that to me. Especially with a query over where it came from. I might be buying myself trouble, mightn't I? However, I'd like to oblige you. I'll give you thirty selenicas for it. And it's part of the deal, of course, that if questions are asked I don't know anything about it."

Andreas said, "That's not fair. You should give us what it's really worth."

"What I *should* do," said Alexis, "is confiscate the coin, pending inquiries. Would you prefer that to thirty selenicas?"

"At least give us fifty," said Andreas in a desperate attempt to bargain.

"Thirty selenicas. Take it or leave it."

"Oh, take it!" said Eleni. Her skin felt slimy, as if the very presence of the steward were smearing it. "I just want to get away from here!"

The steward left the room, and came back a minute

later with a small leather bag. From it he emptied out a little pile of silver coins, which he pushed across the table toward Eleni. Andreas intercepted and counted them. "There's only twenty-eight," he said.

"Those are all the selenicas I have in the house."

"But you said you'd give us thirty."

Alexis shrugged his shoulders. "I can't give you what I haven't got," he said. "You don't have to take them. Please yourselves."

"Pick them up," Eleni said to Andreas. "I thought we'd be cheated, and we have been."

"Now, now," the steward said. "Remember, you're relying on me to keep this matter private. It isn't wise to speak to me like that." But he was still smiling as he showed them to the door.

Nikos was standing in the passageway outside the business room. He stood back to let them pass, grinning as they went by, but didn't say anything.

"I didn't like the look on Nikos's face," said Andreas when the door of the steward's house had closed behind them. "Do you think he was listening?"

Eleni said, "There's a lot of things about this that I don't like. I don't like keeping things dark, and I don't like Mikele looking after his own skin, and I don't like having to do deals with Alexis."

"It's not like the stories of people setting out on quests," Andreas agreed. "But the stories leave a lot out, don't they?"

"Seems to me," said Eleni, "that the sooner we're on

our way now, the better. We should get some food together tomorrow and start at crack of dawn the day after. How about that?"

"That's fine," Andreas said; and then, a little later, "Oh, no. Look who's come after us!"

It was Nikos.

"Don't go so fast!" he said. "I want to talk to you. Sit down here on the grass."

"Who says we want to talk to *you*?" inquired Eleni.

"You will in a minute," said Nikos. He settled himself comfortably. "Are you going to tell me what you're up to? Or shall I guess?"

Eleni and Andreas were both silent. Nikos said, "I know you got money from my father. Twenty-eight selenicas."

Eleni said, "What if we did?"

"You've no use for twenty-eight selenicas on this island. What is there to buy with money like that? Nothing. I reckon that if you want twenty-eight selenicas, you're going off-island. Right?"

"If we were," said Andreas, "would it be anything to do with you?"

"Of course it would. You're in my crew. We'd be two short."

Nikos grinned.

"I don't care that much," he said. "Finding crews is Yannis's problem, not mine. But let me guess where you're going. You're going to Gold Island, aren't you? If you can make it, that is. The streets of Malama paved with gold and all that. Am I right?"

"We're not telling you anything," Andreas said.

"You may as well tell me. Listen, Andreas, I won't try to stop you. Wish I could come, in fact. It's what I dream of, going to Gold Island. But I'd never get away with it, being the steward's son. They'd be after me in no time at all."

"Too bad," said Eleni unsympathetically. "We'll tell you what it's like when we get back."

"You *are* going, then!" Nikos said. "Gave yourself away, didn't you?"

Andreas frowned. If it had been in Eleni's nature to apologize for anything, she'd have apologized to Andreas. As it was, she looked down at the ground and said nothing. Nikos went on, "What if I tell?"

Eleni had had enough. "Oh, tell who you like and go to the underworld!" she said.

"You *are* one of the boys, aren't you!" Nikos said, half admiring. "Swearing and all!" And then, "That was a joke, about telling. I'm not against you kids, honestly I'm not. I'm going to *help* you."

"I'll believe that when I see it."

"You *will* see it. Now listen. How do you reckon you'll get across the strait to Sideros?"

"That's our business," said Andreas.

"You can't swim it, that's for sure. Too far, and too much current. Steal a boat? But there's only half a dozen boats up there at Stony Point. The fishermen guard them, and move their gear out of them at night. Not a hope. So you must be relying on Tonios to ferry you. Well, I've known Tonios for years. My cousin's a neighbor of his.

45

Tonios'll take anyone across who has two selenicas, and he knows the strait like his own backyard. But if you think you can pay him to keep quiet, you can think again. He'll take your money and give you away just the same. You might as well *tell* everybody which way you've gone."

"So what are you suggesting?" asked Andreas.

"I told you, I'm going to help you. This cousin of mine has a boat, too, a nippy little sailboat. I can take you across the strait, first thing in the morning, and bring the boat straight back. Nobody'll know anything about it. My cousin'll keep quiet, just as I will."

Eleni and Andreas were silent. Nikos said, "Well, what's worrying you?"

Andreas said, "That strait's dangerous. Are you sure you can do it?"

"Sure I can. I've done it dozens of times. Well, three or four times, at least. And you know I can handle a boat."

There was another silence. Nikos said crossly, "Don't you trust me?"

Andreas was tactfully silent, but Eleni said, "No."

Nikos said, "Oh, *you*, Eleni! Trust you to be awkward! You ought to know me by now. We've had a few words, I admit, but I don't mean any harm. Tell you the truth, Eleni, I quite *like* you. I've talked about you to my dad, and he's worried that I might like you too much."

"Oh, yes?" said Eleni skeptically. "Then why do you want to get rid of me? What's in it for you?"

Nikos said, "There isn't anything in it for me. You're doing something I've always wanted to do, and I'd like to help you, that's all. As a friend."

Andreas said slowly, "I think you do want to get rid of us, Nikos. I think you don't like Eleni because she's a better helmsman, and you don't like me because I'm cleverer than you are."

For a moment Nikos looked angry. Then he said, with an effort, "If that's what you want to believe, believe it. Maybe you'll be grateful to me when you're safe at the other side."

Andreas said to Eleni, hesitantly, "I think we should take him up on it."

Eleni was relieved by the explanation Andreas had offered. If Nikos wanted to be rid of them as much as they wanted to be rid of him, then perhaps it was logical that he should help them get away.

"All right," she said. "We'll take a chance."

By the time Nikos left them, they had agreed to meet at Stony Point at dawn, two days later. The tide would then be low and the crossing easiest. Back at Molybdos village, the *Seahawk* would be sitting in the sandy harbor, unable to put to sea until the tide had risen; by that time Nikos would have hurried back and be ready to report for duty. He would claim to have no idea why Eleni and Andreas weren't there, and rather than lose a day's fishing Klito would sail without them. That would give them the best possible start.

"And nobody will know which way you've gone," added Nikos. "They'll probably think you've eloped together and you're tucked away in a cave at the back side of the island, having fun." He winked. "You'll lose your reputation, Eleni."

"You needn't think I care about *that!*" said Eleni, but Andreas blushed.

Afterward Eleni said to Andreas, "I still don't trust him, do you?"

Andreas said, "I think if he was going to give us away he'd just *do* it, not carry on like this. Anyway, we're going to have to trust a lot of people before we've finished. And above all, we have to trust the Living God."

"You're better at that than I am," Eleni said.

·V·

ELENI AWOKE THE NEXT morning feeling uneasy. After the first enthusiasm for her quest, and the determination that had seen her through the following days, came chilling doubts and fears. She didn't feel at all heroic. Wasn't the whole venture a wild-goose chase? Did she really think she could intercede with the Living God, if indeed he existed? Surely she'd parted with the cherished gold coin to no purpose at all. It served her right that she'd been cheated.

Along with the fears came pangs of guilt about leaving Anasta and Milos. There had never been much warmth in her relationship with her mother; but Anasta had fed and reared her, and was finding it harder and harder to till the plot of land. Anasta would miss her. And Milos—disabled, bitter, and often in pain—seemed to have lost interest in helping himself or anyone else. He hung around the cottage most of the day. In the evenings he went to the tavern, where Dinos, in exchange for his possessions, or on promise of future payment, or simply out of pity, would allow him enough wine to forget his troubles.

Eleni surprised Anasta by showing signs of affection. The evening before she was due to leave, she embraced her mother, and the strangeness of the feeling of Anasta's thin body in her arms made Eleni realize that it was the first embrace in many months.

That night she had to stay awake. She had arranged to meet Andreas at the headman's house as soon as it was safe to do so. Stony Point was five rough miles away. The villagers of Molybdos worked hard, and Andreas was sure his father and family would soon be sound asleep. Eleni knew that Anasta, though she would wake promptly at dawn, was unlikely to stir before then. The last person to bed was likely to be Milos, when he came home from the tavern, and she wanted a final word with him before she went.

It seemed a long time before Milos came, but at last Eleni heard him stumble into the cottage and grope his way, cursing, to his corner of the floorspace. He half fell to the ground and pulled his blanket over himself.

"Milos!" she whispered.

"Uh?"

"I wish you'd take care of yourself."

"Uh?"

"And our mother."

"What? What you say?"

Eleni had meant to be gentle with him, but patience wasn't her strong point. She hissed crossly, "Can't you stay sober and do *something* to keep things going, you useless lump?"

"Uh?"

Milos rolled over and started snoring. Anasta, in the other corner, moved in her sleep, and Eleni gave up. She lay, quiet and wide awake, until she was sure the others were settled, then crept softly from the room. The headman's house was at the other end of the village. Eleni skirted the backs of cottages rather than walking along the street. Somewhere a dog barked, and for a minute her heart beat fast, but silence returned.

She was afraid that, in spite of his assurances, Andreas might have fallen asleep, but when she reached his father's house he was in the doorway, waiting for her. For a moment he took her hand, which was something he'd never dared to do before, and she was comforted by the touch. Then they set off along the cart track that led over the hill and away to Stony Point.

Eleni still wore her fisherman's garb, and the twenty-eight selenicas were tucked away in a little pouch. Andreas had food wrapped up in a piece of cloth: bread, goat's-milk cheese, and a little dried fish. He also had three silver selenicas and a few copper pennies, which he had earned or been given. There was a southerly breeze,

and a rind of old moon emerged from time to time between clouds.

"*That* couldn't be better, anyway," said Andreas.
"Fine sailing weather, if it stays like this."

They walked mostly in silence. The track was broad but
uneven, repaired again and again with crudely broken
stones unkind to bare feet; sometimes they walked alongside it. It curved around hillsides, sometimes rising and
sometimes dipping, but gradually working its way upward.
Occasionally they had to tread through a stream. Eleni
grew tired, but had no difficulty in keeping going; she felt
as if she were walking in a dream. She wasn't hungry; she
didn't want to talk, or even to think.

The sky was lightening and birdsong beginning as they
trudged through the heather-clad highlands of northeast-
ern Molybdos. As they came around the shoulder of a hill,
the sun rose out of the sea. Below them was the descent
to Stony Point, then the strait, then, on their right, the
rocky north coast of Sideros, receding into the distance.
Soon afterward Andreas grabbed Eleni's hand.

"Look!" he cried. "The mountain!"

Eleni screwed up her eyes against the sun and searched
the horizon, looking for the frail distant shape of Mount
Ayos, but she couldn't see it. Andreas watched her face
eagerly.

"It must be too near the sun," she said.

"No, it isn't. See that farthest headland? Now look a
little bit to the left of that. You see it now?"

Eleni's eyesight was excellent. She could see an early

fishing boat, out already from one of the hamlets along the Sideros coast; she could see the hamlet itself, nestling into a cove, several miles away. But she couldn't see the Holy Mountain. She turned to Andreas, whose face shone with joy.

"It's an omen!" he declared. "A good omen! When you see the mountain, it's always a sign that things are going well. You do see it, don't you, Eleni?"

A tart remark rose to Eleni's lips. She was on the point of telling him he saw what he wanted to see. But at the last moment she swallowed her words; she hadn't the heart to disappoint him.

"Yes, I see it," she lied.

"It puts fresh energy into you, doesn't it?" Andreas said. He realized he was still holding Eleni's hand and dropped it, embarrassed. Then, at a brisker pace, he led the way ahead.

The track was leading downhill now, but still with many twists and turns. The next time Stony Point came into view, it was much nearer. It had no harbor, but there was a sandy inlet through which a stream ran out to sea, and half a dozen small boats were drawn up on the sand. The sail of one of them was flapping in the breeze with a series of audible slaps. Close by was a familiar figure.

"He's there!" Andreas said.

Nikos hailed them cheerfully.

"Where've you been all day?" he inquired; then, without waiting for an answer, "Have some breakfast." He took bread and sausage and some dried figs from a leather pouch, and shoved food across to them. Eleni's eyes gleamed at the sight of the sausage; it was a rare delicacy on Molybdos at the best of times. But then, Nikos was the steward's son.

Andreas was looking uneasily out at the strait. You could see from here that there was a current. A patch of seaweed was being carried past.

"Tide's still on the ebb," said Nikos. "We just have to allow for it. Dead easy when you know how. Here, try a drop of this." He had wine in a leather bottle.

"I'll stick to water," said Andreas.

"There's plenty in the stream."

Andreas and Eleni drank. Andreas said, "We want to get on our way, Niko. The sooner the better."

"Don't panic. Be like me, take it easy." But Nikos got up and put away the remains of the meal. They slid the boat over the sand and into the water, then scrambled on board. Before Nikos could get a grip on sheet and tiller, the little boat was being swept northward toward the open sea.

Nikos laughed at Eleni's alarmed face.

"I told you, take it easy," he said. "It's always like this. It's the current. I'm allowing for it." He brought the boat closer to the wind, and laughed again at his passengers' faces as the boat heeled.

"Hold tight!" he yelled, his voice carried away.

Eleni was watching the Sideros shore. Though they weren't yet far across the strait, the coast was racing past them. She was thinking that they might have been wiser to pay for the ferryman's skill and experience. But glancing across at Andreas, she saw that his expression was serene. He had placed his trust in the Living God.

Moments later the wind dropped. "Come on, come on!" Nikos exhorted it, and to his companions he said, "It's always a bit tricky just here." A minute later it sprang up again, this time from dead ahead. Nikos could make no headway toward the Sideros shore.

"No good trying to tack in this current," he called. "We'll keep pointing and let it carry us. The tide'll turn soon, and we'll come back on it. Don't look so scared, Eleni. This is always happening."

The landing place on Sideros was now sweeping past, across their bows. Though still pointing at Sideros, the little boat was moving out to sea. Once it was past the land, the force of the current was diffused, and the boat's progress slowed.

"Tide must be turning," Nikos said. "We can start tacking now." And slowly, tack by tack, Sideros began to draw nearer. But the wind was shifting again, and the current was running the opposite way from its previous one. The southward tacks grew longer and the northward ones made little progress. Soon the boat was being carried downwind, back through the strait. The boom swung across with a sickening jerk; Andreas and Eleni had no warning and barely time to duck. The Sideros coast, now close at hand, was gliding past them yet again, and the landing place was coming into view once more. Nikos, no longer laughing, tried desperately to head up into the wind, heeling the boat perilously and hanging with all his strength to sheet and helm. A sudden gust whipped both of them from his grasp and sent him sprawling on the floor of the boat. A wave came over the gunwale and he was lying in water, choking.

With the sail released, the boat righted itself and went with the current. The landing place, a patch of seaweedy sand among black, tumbled rocks, was approaching and would soon be passed. Eleni leaped across Nikos for the helm, and her free hand found the sheet. She never knew quite what she did next, but an instinct for the right thing saved her; the boat shot across the last few yards of the strait and wedged its bow between a couple of rocks.

The current was tugging at it, threatening every moment to send it careering away again. Eleni yelled, "Jump!" Nikos, still waterlogged, couldn't jump. Eleni dropped everything, and she and Andreas helped him to drag himself, coughing and spluttering, over the bow. He wriggled, retching all the way, over sharp and slippery rocks to the sand. Andreas followed, and Eleni went last, taking a perilous leap from the boat as it was swept away. All three, amazingly, were safe on the sandy patch. Andreas still had his package of food, and Eleni had her pouch with the twenty-eight selenicas, but there hadn't been a hope of hanging on to the boat. Wind and tide were stronger by far than they were. Now, lightened by their departure and with sail once more flapping loose, the boat was being carried swiftly southward and out of sight.

Andreas said, "Thank the Living God for Eleni, that's all I can say."

Nikos recovered his breath and his composure. "It was bad luck for me at the end, that's all," he said. "I couldn't have known there'd be a gust like that last one. And what about the boat? Eleni lost it. We wouldn't have lost it if *I* hadn't been out of action, I can tell you!"

Eleni drew herself up.

"You stupid, incompetent clot!" she said. "You nearly drowned the lot of us! I hope I never see you again!"

Nikos, outraged, raised a hand as if to clout her. Then it fell to his side, and his expression of fury gave place to a grin. "You'll be seeing a lot of me," he said. "I'm coming with you!"

Eleni stared at him in horror. "You are not!" she declared emphatically.

Nikos grinned again. "I've no choice," he said. "I can't get back to Molybdos."

"Course you can! You can wave your shirt in the air or something. They'll see you from the other shore, sooner or later. Serve you right if you have to wait. We're off!"

Nikos said, "What will I tell my cousin about his boat?"

"That's your problem," said Eleni.

Andreas asked, "Did he really say you could borrow it?"

"As a matter of fact, no. I didn't ask him. He'd have refused. It'd have been the old story, 'The strait's too dangerous.' So I took it without asking. He'll be hopping mad. But the boat won't come to any harm, you know. It'll drift back and forward till it's found or it runs ashore."

"You *have* to go back," said Andreas. "They'll find the empty boat and they'll think we're all drowned."

"No, they won't. There'll be no bodies washed up. All we have to do is get out of the way, quick."

Suspicion flashed into Eleni's mind.

"Did you *ever* intend to go back to Molybdos?" she demanded.

"Well, to tell you the truth," said Nikos, grinning once more, "I didn't. I'm for Malama and seeing a bit of life!"

"What would you do if you got to Malama?" inquired Andreas.

"I can sing, can't I? I'm really good, you know. You should hear what the sailors say who come into Dinos's place. Best they've ever heard, they say. More than one of them's told me I could make my fortune in Malama, with a voice like I have. Well, it's up to me to prove it, and I know I can. If I have to, I'll start by singing in the street. As for you two, well, I don't know what you're planning to do there, and I'm not asking any questions. I'm just coming with you for the company."

"You're not," said Eleni. "We don't want your company, thank you very much."

"I *am*," said Nikos. "You can't stop me, can you?"

"Your clothes are all soaked."

"Trust a woman to think of a thing like that. I'm not

58

worrying. They'll dry on my back. Look, the sun's coming up fast. It's going to be a warm day. And the sooner we get moving, the better. Come on, fellows."

He strode away up the path that led from the landing patch toward the cliff top. Eleni stayed where she was. Nikos halted and called back, "Are you going to wait all day? Somebody'll see you. Come on!"

"He's right. We'd better go," said Andreas. "And Eleni, there's a purpose in all things. The Living God may have *sent* him to help us."

"So far as I'm concerned," said Eleni, "he needn't have bothered." But she moved off, all the same. Andreas walked beside her, while Nikos still strode ahead. He was singing now, in his rough but tuneful voice, a song of which the refrain was "We'll all go together to the end of the road."

· VI ·

Two BROAD CART TRACKS led from the top of the cliff. One went eastward, the other to the south. There wasn't any doubt that the eastward track was the right one. It could be seen ahead for some distance, winding away from the coast over grassy upland on which sheep grazed. There were no people in sight, and there was very little cover, only a few bent and stunted trees.

"We'll be visible from here for a long time," said Nikos, "so hurry." He still strode ahead, singing from time to time and in obvious high spirits. Eleni and Andreas followed. Eleni was full of resentment; it seemed to her that Nikos had not only thrust his company on them but appointed himself the leader. All the same, they stepped out smartly, anxious to get as far as possible from Molybdos.

The first sign they saw of human habitation was a tiny wayside hamlet: a huddle of half a dozen cottages beside the track. As they approached it, a gaunt, hollow-eyed man came out of a tumbledown stable, leading a donkey. "Good morning, friend!" Nikos called. But the man made no response, giving them a long, hard stare as they went past. Looking back, Eleni saw that he was still staring after them.

"Nice fellow." said Nikos sardonically. "They're a surly lot on Sideros. Ignorant and superstitious, too, my dad says."

"Maybe they're not used to strangers," said Andreas.

"He took a good look at us," said Eleni. "He'll remember us. The sooner we're off this track, the better."

Most of the cottages that made up the hamlet seemed derelict, their doorframes gaping empty, but outside one of them a couple of naked children were squatting in the dirt. They called out in small, whining voices, begging for food.

Andreas said, "We didn't eat our breakfast, did we?" He drew out his package of food and offered it to the children. They grabbed with both hands, cramming bread and cheese into their mouths. A woman with a small baby in her arms came to the door, watched for a short while with apparent lack of interest, then suddenly dived between the two children to seize the last small chunk of bread, which she devoured with the same greedy urgency.

"They're starving!" Andreas said. "Have you any more food, Niko?"

"No," said Nikos. "We ate it all."

Andreas groped in his clothing and found a selenica, which he gave to the woman. She stared at it for a moment in surprise, then shuffled off with it into the cottage without a word. Almost at once an elderly woman and a middle-aged man appeared from what had looked like empty cottages, holding out their hands. Andreas gave each of them a selenica and scattered a few pennies for the children to scramble for. Then he smiled happily and said, "That's it. All I have. I'm as poor as they are now."

Eleni said crossly, "I suppose that makes you feel good. You're crazy. If *I* threw money around like that we wouldn't get far, would we?"

"Don't worry," said Nikos. "I have lots of money. Look!" He put a hand inside his still-sodden tunic. Then he cried in an agonized tone, "It's gone! Who's taken it?"

"Nobody's been near you!" Eleni said. "I didn't know you *had* money!"

Nikos had taken his tunic off, and was feeling frantically all over it, then over the rest of his clothing.

"Let's have a look." Eleni said. There was a pocket sewn into the inside of the tunic, but it was empty.

"Your money's fallen out, Niko. Must have happened while we were dragging you from the boat. Was it much?"

"Twenty helions."

"Twenty *helions*! That's a fortune! How'd you come to have twenty helions?"

"Well . . . It was borrowed from my dad. To set me up in Malama."

"Did he *know* you'd borrowed it?"

"No."

"Oh, for the Living God's sake! Your father'd chase us to the underworld for that amount of money!"

"We'd better go back to the strait," said Nikos, "and see if we can find it."

"Some hope." said Eleni. "The tide'll be higher by now."

"And even if we found it," said Andreas uneasily, "it'd still be your dad's money."

Nikos looked from one of them to the other. He was close to tears. Suddenly he seemed more an overgrown boy than a young man.

Eleni said decisively, "Niko, *I'm* not turning back. We can't give up the start we have. *You* can go back if you like. In fact, if I was you I'd go right back home to Molybdos."

"I *can't* go home," Nikos said, "with the boat and the money lost. My dad would slay me! I *have* to go on. When I get to Malama, I'll make good. I'll pay him back in the end. But right now I have nothing. Not a penny."

To her own surprise, Eleni felt sorry for him. His confidence had disappeared with the helions, and now he seemed pathetic.

"You can come with us if you like," she said, "and take your chance. It's good *one* of us has a bit of common sense."

She set off again, leading the way along the track. The people to whom Andreas had given his money had disappeared, but the gaunt man they'd first seen, now without his donkey, was standing silently in front of one of the cottages; when they'd gone some distance and Eleni looked around, he was still there, watching them.

Nikos, dispirited, now trailed a little way behind the other two. Andreas said to Eleni, thoughtfully, "I wonder what's happened, for that place to be in such a desperate state."

"Same as has happened to Molybdos, I reckon," said Eleni.

"The fact is," said Andreas, "things are disastrous. We owe it to the people to go on."

"I don't owe anything to anybody," said Eleni. "But I've started, and I'm not stopping now."

After a while the track came to the coast again and ran close to the cliff top, heading eastward along Sideros's north shore. The cliffs grew higher, and eventually the track had to skirt a hill that dropped sheer to the sea. This was a relief to the walkers, for once they were around the hillside, they were no longer in view from far behind. And soon a wooded valley lay ahead of them. A stream ran through it, and where the stream reached the seashore were the houses of a village, much bigger than the tiny hamlet they'd passed before. The track wound downhill toward the village. Eleni and Andreas stopped to think.

"Maybe we should steer clear of the village," Eleni said. "We don't want to leave a trail."

Nikos caught up with them.

"I'm tired," he said. "Could we have a rest?"

He was asking Eleni's permission. For the time being

64

at least, he'd relinquished the leadership. He mopped his forehead.

They had walked quite a long way by now, and none of them had had any sleep the night before. And there were plenty of places in the woodland where they could lie low.

"Seems to me," Eleni said, "that we'd be safest if we traveled at night. So why don't we stay here till dark?"

They left the track and made their way through the woods to the stream, at a point well above the first houses. Here they found a quiet, shaded spot on the bank. They were all thirsty, and drank from the stream before stretching out on the bank.

"Whoever wakes first, wake the others," Eleni said.

They hadn't realized how tired they were. The sun was low in the sky by the time Eleni woke. Andreas was sweetly asleep, a slight smile on his face. She roused him gently. Nikos lay on his back with his mouth open, snoring. She didn't feel like being gentle with Nikos, and dug him sharply in the ribs.

Nikos sat up, rubbing his eyes, and said, "I'm hungry."

"So what are you going to do about it?" Eleni asked. "You going to catch a rabbit?"

Nikos looked crestfallen, and said nothing. Andreas, awake now, was also silent. Eleni became aware of the hollowness of her own stomach.

"All right," she said. "I won't let you starve if I can help it. We'll buy food in the village. If there's anyone who'll sell it to us, that is. I guess this is where I start spending my selenicas. Come along. It'll be dark soon."

When the others caught up with Eleni, she was at the far edge of the patch of woodland, looking out from it at a cottage that stood by itself, away from the village. It was a humble-enough dwelling, with low roof and unglazed window. Behind it was a vegetable garden; hens pecked in the yard, and a little distance away a goat was tethered. An old woman with a basket was picking something in the garden, and as they watched she hobbled to the house, went in, and closed the door behind her. Eleni looked across at her companions. Andreas nodded. Nikos said, "If we wait until after dark, we can help ourselves. And milk the goat."

Eleni asked, "Would you do that on Molybdos?"

"No, of course I wouldn't. But we know everybody there. They're our neighbors."

"My mother has a plot of land, and she's had it done to her, once or twice. And you know what I call people who do a thing like that to poor folk? Shits, that's what I call them. Shits."

Nikos went crimson.

"Let's see if she can sell us something," Eleni said. She groped beneath her tunic and extracted a selenica from her pouch. Then she led the way to the cottage door and knocked. Nothing happened, and she knocked again, harder.

"Let me have a go," said Nikos, recovering. He battered at the door with his fists. It was opened, cautiously, an inch or two. Andreas said, "Don't be afraid. We're not going to harm you."

The door opened a little farther.

"Who are you? Where are you from?"

The woman was very old and shrunken, with sparse white hair and a brown, deeply wrinkled face. She wore a ragged shift and a shawl, and was barefoot. It was hard to tell what she was saying, because her accent was strange and she had no teeth.

"We're travelers," Andreas said. "We'd like to buy food from you."

"You're not from the lord, then?"

"No."

The door opened wider.

"When young men I don't know come here, they're likely to be from the lord," the old woman said. "But they don't *buy* food these days, they just take it. All they can lay their hands on. I tell them what I think of them, but they just laugh at me. The king wants it from the lord and the lord wants it from us, and none of them care if we live or die. You're *sure* you're not from the lord?"

"We don't know anything about your lord," Eleni said.

The old woman looked hard at her, then said, "I'll take your word for it. But you're not all young men, are you? *You're* a young woman, in spite of the way you're dressed. And no better than you should be, I daresay. Going around openly with two young fellows, and got up like that! What are you all up to?"

67

Andreas said patiently, "We're from Molybdos. We're on our way to Gold Island. And look, we have money."

Eleni produced the selenica. The old woman's eyes widened.

"I don't see many of those these days," she said. "Well, if you're not from the lord and you're not thieves and vagabonds, you can come in."

The cottage was miserably poor, no more than a hovel. It had an earth floor, and a hole in the roof through which smoke escaped. But over a fire was a big iron pot.

"Stew!" said Nikos.

"Yes. It's my supper. And tomorrow's and the day after's as well. I keep that pot going. Mind you, with times being so hard, there's many a day I've nothing to put in it but a few vegetables."

"It smells good, all the same."

"It's better than usual. I killed one of my hens yesterday. She'd stopped laying, poor thing, so she had to go."

Eleni asked, "Could you sell us some stew, to eat now?"

"No, I couldn't. I asked you into my house, didn't I? There's some in this village that'd ask guests to pay for a meal, but I'm not one of them. I stick to the old ways. You can have some stew if you want, but you can't pay for it."

But all the time she spoke the old woman's eyes were on the selenica in Eleni's hand. Andreas started to argue that the stew should be paid for, but Eleni stopped him.

"All right," she said. "We'll take the stew as a gift and buy something from you later."

68

"We'll see," the old woman said. "I don't have much to sell."

She found three bowls, all chipped and cracked, ladled stew into them, and put beside each a hunk of bread. Andreas asked, "Can you spare this?"

The woman said, "I'm all right. Don't ask questions, just get on with it."

Eleni, Andreas, and Nikos sat side by side on a bench at a worn and scratched table, and ate. The stew was hot, savory and comforting. The old woman sat on a stool opposite them and watched. When they finished, she took the bowls and, without a word, refilled them.

Nikos, the loss of his helions temporarily forgotten, sat back replete and patted his stomach. "That was great," he said.

The old woman, who hadn't smiled all the time they were in the cottage, said dourly, "Young folk are like goats and chickens. They need feeding properly if they're to thrive." And then, "My children are all dead, and my husband too, but I've a grandson your age, if he's still alive. I don't rightly know. He was taken last spring, for a soldier, and I haven't heard of him since. They tell me there's a war."

"There *was*," said Andreas. "It's over for the time being. Didn't you know? We lost."

"I don't hear much. Nobody tells an old woman anything. What happened to the men?"

"Those who were wounded came back. At least, they did to Molybdos. I expect they did to Sideros, too."

"Were there many killed, do you know?"

"There were some, I think," said Andreas cautiously.

"And those that weren't killed or wounded?"

Andreas looked at the other two, opened his mouth and closed it again, unable to bring himself to speak. Nikos said, "Go on, we got to tell her. Truth is, Granny, according to what those who came back said, some were taken prisoner and sold into slavery. And those that weren't captured were kept in the army, or else put to work in the mines, on Orichalcos."

There was a long silence. The old woman bowed her head in her hands. At last she said, "If he's in the army, there's hope. But if they sent him to the orichalc mines, I pray to the Living God he's dead." Her eyes were full of tears.

Eleni got up, went to the old woman and put her arms round her, but couldn't think of anything to say. Andreas asked, "Do you have faith in the Living God?"

"I believe in him. At least, I think I do. I always have. But it doesn't get easier. What's hardest is to think he *cares* about what happens to the likes of us."

Andreas said to Eleni, "I want to tell her what we're doing. May I?"

Eleni thought for a moment, then said, "I can't see that it'll do any harm. We haven't been told *not* to tell. And remember we haven't told Nikos yet."

Andreas declared impressively, "Eleni is the Messenger. She's on a mission to the Living God!"

The hearers' eyes grew round as Andreas embarked on

70

the theme. Eleni felt foolish and embarrassed at first, half expecting to hear snickers or jeers from Nikos. But he sat in silence, impressed by Andreas's sincerity. When Andreas finished, Nikos looked at Eleni with wonder and respect.

"Well, I always thought Eleni might do *anything*!" he said.

The old woman made the gesture of homage to the god. Then she asked, "Is it only Molybdos that the Living God'll save?"

Andreas considered the point, then said, "If he's saving people from oppression, I don't see why he should draw a line between Molybdos and here. It's my belief that when Eleni reaches him, he will save us all."

"Then bless you, my dear!" the old woman said to Eleni. "And as for a girl being Messenger, I can't for the life of me see why not. It's time we women took a hand, when you see what the men have done. Yes, I know I shouldn't say such things, but when you get to my age you don't mind shocking people so much. You shall have all I can give you when you set out from here. Which will be in the morning, I hope. It's getting dark already."

"The dark's the time we should travel," said Andreas.

Eleni nodded. "We'll lie low in the daytime," she said. "And we've had a good sleep today already. We'll be on our way."

Nikos seemed still awed by Andreas's revelation. He accepted Eleni's decision to leave without question. The old woman gave them hard-boiled eggs, bread, and vegetables. She tried to refuse payment, but Eleni thrust the selenica upon her, and a second one as well.

"Two silver selenicas!" she said. "That's far too much. But . . . wait a moment, my dear. Let me give you something to take on your journey. I don't know what it is, but I have a feeling it's special. And maybe it's specially for you."

She gave Eleni a disc, hung on a chain. The disc was the size of a golden helion, but it didn't look valuable. It was a thin, round black stone, like an unusually flat pebble. Finely engraved on it was the image of a root and stem from which arose a bud, a flower, and a fruit, all at once.

"Pretty, isn't it?" the old woman said. "I hung it on the chain myself, but I couldn't bring myself to wear it. It was as if I knew it wasn't meant for me. Somehow I feel it'll be right on you, though."

Andreas gasped. "You know what that is?" he asked, astonished; then, looking at the three blank faces, "No, of course you wouldn't. I only know through being a priest's helper. It's the secret symbol of the Living God, for whom all time is one. In fact the Time All One is what it's called. Wherever did you find it?"

"At the top of the hill, near here, a week or two ago. I suddenly felt I had to go up there. And I don't know why, because when you get to my age, and with rheumatism like mine, you think twice before you start hill climbing. But I had this urge, and I said to myself, well, maybe it's the last time I'll ever do it, I'm not getting any younger, so off I went. And when I got there I started looking around on the ground, I don't know why. And there it was, tucked away between a couple of stones. It was as if it drew my eyes to it."

"You were *meant* to find it!" Andreas declared.

The others were silent. Andreas went on, "Can you see Mount Ayos from that hill?"

"Yes, as a matter of fact you can, some days. Usually after rain."

"I knew it! There must have been a shrine there, sometime. This is a special, sacred thing. Our priest on Molybdos doesn't have one. Only the inner priests on Gold Island and those called for special service to the god have the right to wear it. And now we have a wearer. You see that tiny lettering round the edge. Know what it says?"

His hearers shook their heads. None of them could read.

"It says, 'Who bears me shall see the Living God.' "

Reverently, Andreas placed the chain around Eleni's neck. The disc slid from view beneath her tunic, but she was conscious of its cool smoothness against her flesh. Nikos and the old woman stood bemused.

"Now do you believe in the Living God?" Andreas demanded.

For a moment Eleni felt again the surge of belief that arose in spite of herself; maybe it *was* her destiny to meet face to face with the Living God. But as swiftly as it had come the belief dwindled away. The thing she'd been given was only a bit of black stuff, and if it had to do with the priesthood, well then, a former shrine was exactly where you'd expect it to be found. For Andreas's sake she'd have liked to answer "Yes" to his question, but honesty prevented her.

"I *nearly* do," she said. "Not quite."

·VII·

THE MOON WAS STILL only a sliver, but the sky was clear
and it wasn't a dark night. There wasn't going to be much
cover. As they left the cottage, Andreas glanced across
toward the point at which they'd left the wood after their
rest. He stiffened. "There's somebody standing there," he
whispered.

Nikos charged in the direction indicated; there was a
rustle of undergrowth. Nikos disappeared into the wood
in pursuit, but emerged two or three minutes later.

"No luck," he said. "There *was* something there, but
it got away."

"I'm sure it was a person," said Andreas.

"Could have been an animal."

"Have you ever seen an animal with a white face
about a person's height from the ground? Somebody was
watching us."

"You're jumpy, Andreas," Nikos said. "Take it easy."

Nikos was recovering his usual swagger. Andreas didn't answer, but still looked uneasy. Eleni said reluctantly, "I think Nikos is right. It's easy to imagine things when you're a bit nervous. Still, we'll watch out."

Beyond the village they rejoined the track. It led back to the cliff top. They were at the beginning of a long bay with a wide sandy beach, and soon there was a narrow path down the cliff.

"Let's walk on the sand," Eleni said. "We won't be so visible there." And for much of the night they trudged along the beach to the sound of the sea and under the shadow of the cliffs. High tide came and went. Toward dawn they came to the end of the beach, at a headland where waves broke against the rocks; a narrow, perilous track led around the cliff face. And at the other side of the headland a village suddenly came into sight. It was the biggest village they'd seen so far, with an enclosed harbor and a sizeable cluster of houses. In the east the sky was lightening. Somewhere a cock crowed and a dog barked. Lamps were coming on in cottage windows.

"Go back," Eleni said. "We'll go around this place, like we did the other."

They retreated around the headland and scrambled precariously to the cliff top. Once in safety and out of sight of the village, they collapsed briefly on the grass, a few feet from the cliff edge, to get their breath.

They were about to move on when scrabbling sounds came from over the cliff. Nikos went to the edge. Eleni and Andreas saw only part of what happened next. There was another figure there; Nikos was grappling with it, and they heard him shout, "Get back, you bastard!" Then the second figure disappeared and Nikos was standing at the edge, looking over. Eleni and Andreas ran to join him. Many feet below them a man was slithering, face to the cliff, grasping for handholds and sending soil down from his searching feet. As they watched, he brought himself to a halt, spreadeagled on the sloping face of the cliff. Recovering, he began to move again, but not upward: He was cautiously working his way down to the path that would have led them to the village.

"Who's he?" demanded Eleni. "What did you do?"

"He's the man we saw yesterday morning, who looked so interested. It must be him who was lurking in the wood, near the old woman's house. He's been following us. And what do you *think* I did? I pushed him back. That dealt with him all right!"

"For the moment," said Andreas. "But you're crazy. You could have killed him."

"Yes, I guess I could," said Nikos. He didn't seem upset by the thought.

"We don't know what he's up to. But if he *is* on our trail, he'll be after us again soon. We'd better get away from here, quick!"

Behind the village was grassland, offering no cover, and now it was daylight.

"We'll have to hide," said Andreas.

"Hide where?"

"Well . . . what's that building over there?"

It was a long, low barn, now leaning over and in a poor state of repair. In the middle of one side was an opening big enough to admit a cart.

"We haven't much choice," Andreas said. "Let's see what's inside."

The building was empty, apart from a pile of old and musty hay. Behind the hay they could conceal themselves after a fashion. They sat in a little group, looking at each other.

"I might have known you'd get us into trouble," Eleni said crossly to Nikos.

"We're not in trouble *yet*," Nikos said. "What about some food?"

Eleni realized that after the night's walk she was hungry. They ate the food the old woman had given them. Nikos took off his tunic, rolled it, and placed it under his head.

"Nothing we can do," he said cheerfully. "I'm going to sleep." And almost at once he was snoring.

It was true that there was nothing to be done except wait for darkness once more and hope not to be discovered in the meantime. Eleni didn't feel at all sleepy. Her heart was thumping, and she feared at any moment to see a shadow fall across the doorway or to hear approaching footsteps. After a while she saw that Andreas's head was nodding, and soon afterward she saw that he too was asleep. She stayed awake, meditating uneasily. It seemed to her that they'd put themselves in a trap. Though, as

Andreas had said, they hadn't much choice. . . . And then, in spite of her fears, she was asleep herself.

She was awakened by a kick in the ribs. A big, burly middle-aged man was standing over her. A second man of about the same age, with a round, amiable face stood beside him. In the doorway was a third, and Eleni recognized him at once as the gaunt-looking man who'd stared at them with such interest in the hamlet they'd first reached.

"On your feet, lad!" the big man said to Eleni. He moved on to Andreas and aimed another kick, but Andreas, quickly awake at the sound of a voice, rolled out of reach and hastily got up.

"Niko!" Andreas called in warning, but Nikos didn't stir until kicked. He sat up, startled and aggressive, and looked around at the three intruders. Then he rose slowly to his feet, put on his tunic, and looked around again.

"Well?" he said.

"Is these they, Greg?" the big man asked.

"Them's 'em," said the gaunt man in the doorway. "And *he's* the one what pushed me over the cliff." He pointed at Nikos.

"Want to make anything of it?" asked Nikos belligerently.

"Now, now, none of that, young feller!" said the big man. "You behave yourself or you'll get clouted. And you know who'll clout you? *I* will." He clenched and raised an enormous fist. "And just in case you got any wrong ideas, there's more of us outside."

"Tell them who you are, Hektor," suggested Greg.

"I will that. I am the headman of this here village. And acting on behalf of the lord, I'm arresting you three lads on suspicion of being vagrants and therefore thieves. And, what's more, on suspicion of being foreigners from Molybdos."

"Molybdos has the same king as Sideros," said Andreas, "so we're not foreigners."

"If you're from Molybdos you're not from these parts," said the big man. "And if you're not from these parts you're foreigners. Stands to reason. And as for *you*"—he turned to Nikos—"you're under arrest for attempted murder as well. Vagrant and foreign *and* a murderer: I reckon you're a bad lot and you need to be made an example of. Right, lads, we'll march 'em down to the lockup."

Nikos eyed the headman challengingly, as if contemplating the possibility of hitting him and making a run for it. But the other two were between him and the doorway, and the voices of more men could be heard from outside. There was clearly no hope of escape. He allowed Hektor to drop a heavy hand on his shoulder and lead him at the head of a little procession into the village main street. Eleni and Andreas, surrounded, could only follow.

The sun was now high in the sky. The lockup was a little stone building, close by the quay. Eleni, Andreas, and Nikos were thrust into it.

"You can cool off in here for a while," said Hektor. "Tomorrow, on behalf of the lord, I shall hear the case and you'll be convicted and sentenced. And in a day or two's time you'll be collected and on your way."

"On our way where?" asked Andreas.

"Never you mind. You'll find out soon enough. If I was you, I wouldn't be in a hurry to know."

The door closed behind the prisoners, and they heard the heavy locking bar drop into its supports. The little building had an earth floor and was totally bare. There was a small opening, far too small for a person to get through, high in one of the walls. When receding footsteps outside had been succeeded by silence, Nikos tried charging the heavy wooden door with his shoulder, but it didn't budge. He settled into a corner, sitting on the floor with his back to the wall.

"Oh, well," he said philosophically, "we'll have to see what happens. If the worst comes to the worst, I can tell them my dad's the steward on Molybdos and knows the lord's agent. They won't dare do anything to me then. They'll be more afraid of that agent than they are of the Living God."

Eleni said indignantly, "You'll save your own skin, eh, Niko?"

"I'm hoping I won't need to do it that way," Nikos said. "It'd be the end of getting to Malama, wouldn't it? I don't want handing over to my dad. We'll find some other way out."

"*What* way out?" demanded Eleni.

"Well . . . What about you? Can't the Living God do something for you?"

Andreas said seriously, "That gives me an idea. Eleni, will you lend me your pendant?"

Eleni had forgotten about the disc the old woman had given her. She slid the chain over her head and passed it to Andreas, who put it around his own neck.

"I think I can do something with this," he said.

"If you can get us out of here with it," said Eleni, "carry on. And the sooner the better. I don't know about you, but I'm thirsty."

They were all thirsty, and grew thirstier as time went by. The hours of imprisonment seemed endless. A mixture of boredom and apprehension made Andreas and Eleni nervous and inclined to snap at each other, but Nikos once again took off his tunic, put it under his head, and went to sleep.

It was evening before Eleni heard the locking bar rattle in its bracket, and the round-faced man who'd accompanied Hektor and Greg to the barn appeared in the doorway. He brought water, a hunk of bread, and another of goat's-milk cheese. His expression seemed friendly enough.

Andreas said, "I thought you'd forgotten all about us."

"No chance of that. But time drags when you're locked up. I know; I was in here for a week once when I was a lad. Stealing fruit from an orchard." He grinned. "I guess I lived it down. I'm deputy headman now. Spyros is my name. Hektor's the chief, of course, and he likes holding court. Does it whenever he gets a chance. He'll be in his element tomorrow."

Andreas asked, "What did he mean by saying we'd be collected and on our way in a day or two?"

Spyros's face clouded. "You really don't know?"

"No."

"Well, it's bad news. Anyone who's found to be a vagrant or vagabond gets handed over to the King's Commissioners."

"And what does *that* mean?"

"You've to serve the King in whatever way they tell you. Earlier this year, when there was fighting on the mainland, it'd have been the army. That wasn't so bad. At least you had a chance of staying alive. But now they send them all to . . . well, I *have* to tell you . . . the orichalc mines. And that's something I wouldn't wish on my worst enemy."

Spyros's expression was troubled. "Fact is, if it was up to me, I wouldn't let it happen to anyone, not for all the gold in Gold Island. But they don't all think like me. It's the bounty that does it."

"What bounty?"

"Anyone who hands a vagrant over gets a bounty. Five helions. That's a useful bit of money. Three vagrants is worth fifteen helions. You can keep a family for a year on fifteen helions, which is what Greg'll get for handing you over. He'll have to give Hektor a bit of it, of course, for convicting you, but what's left is still more than he'll ever make any other way."

"So *that's* why he was trailing us," Andreas said.

"You can't blame him altogether," said Spyros. "He

has a wife and children to keep, and the times are dread-ful."

"The bastard!" said Nikos. "I wish I *had* killed him!" Then, to Spyros, "You say *you* wouldn't do it to anybody. Why not let us escape?"

Spyros looked alarmed.

"I wouldn't dare," he said. "I'd probably finish up in the orichalc mines myself."

Andreas drew the black disc from under his tunic.

"Have you ever seen anything like this before?" he inquired.

Spyros studied it.

"No," he said. "What is it? A lucky charm?"

"It's more than that." Andreas's tone was solemn. Spyros's eyes widened.

"Magic?" he asked. He eyed the disc warily. "It does have a kind of magic look about it."

"It's greater than magic," said Andreas. "That pattern is a sacred symbol. A symbol of the Living God."

Spyros, startled, made the gesture of homage. Andreas went on, "Only those who serve the god may wear it."

"So how do you come to have it?"

"I serve the Living God," said Andreas with dignity. "And by virtue of this emblem, I demand to see your priest. The village has a priest, hasn't it?"

"Oh, sure," said Spyros. "*Anyone* locked up overnight can see the priest, if they ask. It's so they can get forgive-ness for their wickedness. But Theodoros charges for it. Most folk can't afford that. And before he comes, he asks if the prisoner looks able to pay. What shall I say?"

84

"Tell him," said Andreas, "that I carry the Time All One. That will bring him."

Spyros backed out, his eyes still resting uneasily on the disc. The locking bar rattled in the brackets.

Andreas said, "Sorry, Eleni. The medal is yours, not mine. I'll hand it back to you later. But I think I can use it and you can't."

"Don't worry," said Eleni. "Hey, you impressed that fellow, didn't you? He half expected it to jump up and bite him!"

"Villagers are superstitious," said Andreas. "They have more belief in magic than in the Living God."

"Isn't the Living God magic?"

"Someday, Eleni," said Andreas severely, "I will explain the difference to you."

It wasn't long before the priest appeared. He was middle-aged and clean-shaven, with a pale, fleshy face and blue jowls. To the surprise of the prisoners Hektor, looking irritated, had come with him. The priest stretched out his hand at once for the medal. Andreas drew it away, but, holding it firmly between thumb and forefinger, held it so it could be seen. Theodoros peered intently, then backed away, startled.

"That's it," he said. "It's the Time All One, the emblem of the inner priesthood. How do you come to have it?" Then, suspiciously, "Did you steal it?"

"I did not," said Andreas. "I serve the Living God."

"You look too young to be a priest at all, never mind a priest of the inner brotherhood. I know there are a few sprigs of the aristocracy who become inner priests when they're hardly out of their cradles, but you're not one of those."

"I'm not one of those," Andreas said, "but I have entered priest training."

"You have? Prove it. Answer these questions."

The priest rapped out a series of questions. Andreas rapped the answers back at him instantly. Questions and answers rattled alternately on Eleni's ears, so quickly that she could hardly take them in.

"Who is the Living God?"

"He is the source of life and light."

"Where does the Living God reside?"

"In the hearts of men and on the Holy Mountain."

"Where is the Holy Mountain?"

"At the center of the world."

"Where is the center of the world?"

"It is the city of Malama, on the Island of Gold, in the Fortunate Isles."

"What earthly form does the Living God take?"

"The God takes mortal flesh."

"How is the God renewed?"

"By the passage of his spirit from one mortal form to another."

"How is the God's new incarnation known?"

"The God, in mortal voice, names a successor."

"Who are the people of the Living God?"

"The people of the Fortunate Isles."

"Who is the Chief Lay Servant of the God?"

"The King is his Chief Lay Servant."

"What is the duty of the Chief Lay Servant?"

"It is to rule the people in earthly matters."

"Who are the spiritual servants of the God?"

"They are the appointed priesthood."

"Who shall see the Living God face to face?"

"Only the King and those of the inner priesthood, save for one day in the year, when the God shall show himself in mortal form in his city of Malama."

"How shall the common people win the God's approval?"

"They shall obey the King's representatives in earthly matters and the priesthood in spiritual ones."

"Good," said the priest. "You know the approved responses. Who taught them to you?"

"Mikele, the priest on Molybdos. I was—am—his helper."

"I know Mikele. A drunken oaf if ever there was one. *He's* not an inner priest, that's for sure. You can't have got the Time All One by stealing it from him. So how did you get it?"

"It was guided our way," said Andreas with sincerity. "It was guided by the Living God."

The priest turned to the headman.

"These are secret matters," he said. "I cannot have the Time All One discussed in front of common people. You must release the boy to me for questioning. I shall take him to my house for the night."

Hektor had been listening, bewildered, to the exchanges between the priest and Andreas.

"If you say so," he said reluctantly. "What about the other two?"

"You can keep them here. I may need to question them later."

"And the hearing tomorrow morning?"

"Don't begin it until I say so."

"But we want to get on with it. There's bounty involved."

"I can't help that. You'll collect it in the end, I daresay. But you'll have to be patient. You're out of your depth with things like this, Hektor. The Time All One isn't a matter for village headmen and local courts."

"Oh, isn't it? Courts are my business, not yours, however high and mighty you think you are."

"There's no need to take it like that. Look at it this way. It's a matter that could cause trouble. I can't afford to take chances."

Hektor scowled. But after a brief hesitation he said, "All right. The lad goes with you, Theo, on your responsibility. The other two stay here until further notice. Spyros, see there's somebody on guard all night. *I'm* not taking chances either."

Andreas accompanied the priest from the lockup. He waved to the other two as he went.

"Well, he's got *himself* out of here for the time being," said Nikos.

"If he can, he'll get *us* out of here, too," said Eleni. She still lacked faith in the Living God, but she was developing a good deal of faith in Andreas.

·VIII·

ELENI AND NIKOS were left in the lockup with Spyros, who was puzzled but sympathetic.

"I don't know what all that's about," he said. "I'm out of my depth with that kind of thing. Maybe you'll be let out later, like your friend. Nobody'd be happier than me if that happened. But in the meantime, it's up to me to see you don't get away. And I'm telling you straight, you might as well save your efforts, because you haven't a chance. My advice is, try to get some sleep and hope for the best."

He went, and the bar rattled into its brackets on the outside of the door. It was dark in the cell, with only a little light coming through the tiny window, and before long that faded. Eleni sat in a corner with her hands clasped round her knees. In the gloom she couldn't see

Nikos, but after a while he shuffled toward her and put an arm around her shoulders. Eleni thrust it away.

"Eleni. We're in this together. We may as well be pals."

"Speak for yourself," said Eleni. "I didn't choose your company."

"Don't be like that, Eleni. I *like* you, didn't you know? I like you a lot."

Eleni didn't respond. Nikos put his arm around her shoulders again and tried to drag her down beside him on the floor. Eleni jerked herself free. If he went any further, she was going to give him a vicious jab where she knew it would hurt. She wasn't afraid of Nikos.

Nikos seemed to accept the rebuff. He drew away. It was too dark even to see where he was, but after a while she could tell from his breathing that he was asleep. She wished she could sleep herself, but she was too anxious.

As the night went on, it grew cold. Eleni shivered and huddled into her tunic, but the cold worked through to her skin and then, it seemed, to her bones. Nikos, now snoring gently, still slept. He was the only source of warmth. She moved toward him and, reluctantly, lay at his side. He half-woke, put an arm around her, muttered "That's better," and went to sleep again. She was asleep in Nikos's arms when a commotion came at the door of the lockup. There was a shout, followed by the sounds of a scuffle and a sharp cry of pain that suddenly broke off. Then the door burst open, moonlight poured in, and Andreas was there.

———

"It's Spyros!" he cried, in an agonized tone. "I've hit him on the head! Laid him out! I may have killed him!"

Nikos leaped to his feet, instantly awake and alert. Spyros's inert form lay just outside the doorway. There was no one else around. Nikos made a swift inspection.

"He's not dead," he said. "Just unconscious. Shove him inside and bar the door. And then let's get away from here!"

Andreas stood shaking, unable for a moment to move. Eleni picked up Spyros's feet, and she and Nikos heaved him into the lockup. They dragged Andreas outside and dropped the bar into place behind them.

"Now run as if all the underworld were after you!" Nikos urged; and he raced away up the village street. Eleni followed at once and, looking around, saw that Andreas had recovered and was running after her.

The village was silent except for their own footfalls. There wasn't much cover in its immediate neighborhood, but the hills weren't far away. Eleni, Andreas, and Nikos left the broad coastal path and headed away from the sea: first across open country, then scrubby moorland. Their pace slackened until they were walking and trotting by turns, but there wasn't any sign of pursuit, and when the first signs of dawn came they were in the hills, away from any track or signs of habitation. They followed a stream toward its source and saw ahead of them what looked like a way through to the east. It was deceptive; beyond its apparent high point lay another, and beyond that another. They plodded onward, silent, losing any sense of time, needing all their breath and energy to keep going and still fearing pursuit. At last, far up in the pass, with a long view to their rear and no one in sight behind, they came to a place where several great boulders sprawled, and sat in the shelter of one of them.

Eleni, giving way at last to her curiosity, asked Andreas eagerly, "What happened?"

Nikos added, "Yes, that was great, Andreas, the way you got us out of there. Tell us all about it."

Andreas didn't look entirely happy.

"I never hit anyone like that before," he said. "Not in all my life. And it was Spyros. I liked him."

"He'll be none the worse," said Nikos cheerfully. "Though I wish it had been the other fellow, the one who'd have sold us into the mines for five helions each."

"But how did you get away from the priest, Andreas?" asked Eleni.

"It wasn't too hard. You know what he was up to? He wanted me as his helper. He hasn't got one at present. As soon as he got me away from the other lot, he turned all nice and fatherly. Gave me a good supper, out in the courtyard, and a room of my own in the house. And it's a lovely house—better than any we have on Molybdos except maybe your dad's, Niko. He said I was a clever boy and I'd learn more from him than I ever would from Mikele. I didn't trust him a bit, but I played along with him."

"And what about the medal?" Eleni asked.

"The Time All One? He didn't say much about that—

———

92

said we'd talk about it later—but I reckon he had his eye on it all the same. I think he wanted it for himself."

"He gave you a room but didn't lock you in it?"

"He thought he didn't need to. He gave me some wine after supper. If I'd drunk it, it would have laid me out till morning. But I've learned more from Mikele than he thinks, especially the medicine. I knew by sniffing it what he'd done. I tipped it into his herb bed while he wasn't looking. Then all I had to do was pretend to be asleep but stay awake. Easy."

"I bet it wasn't *that* easy," said Eleni.

"He came in once and had a look at me. Then I suppose he went to bed. I waited a good long time, then I got up and let myself out. I'd seen a big heavy pestle that he used for mixing medicines, and I picked it up on the way."

"You knew you'd need it, eh?" said Nikos admiringly.

"Well, I'm not sure," said Andreas. His manner had livened up as he told the story, but now he looked worried again. "Priests are supposed to be men of peace."

"You're not a priest yet."

"I've vowed service to the Living God. And I don't *know* what made me pick that thing up. But anyway I did pick it up, and I went straight to the lockup, and there was Spyros, sitting with his back to the door, and I think he was dozing. Anyway, he wasn't watching out. And something suddenly told me to hit him on the head. And I did. If I'd stopped to think, I couldn't have done it. . . . I hope I didn't kill him."

"Course you didn't!" said Nikos. "And hey, won't that

93

priest be in trouble! I wish I could see all their faces this morning!"

"It was a bad thing to do," said Andreas. "I yielded to an evil impulse."

"Andreas," said Eleni thoughtfully, "what if it *wasn't* an evil impulse? What if it was the Living God himself that put it into your head?"

For a moment Andreas looked astonished at the idea. Then an uncertain smile dawned on his face.

"I suppose it could have been," he said.

"Well, you were carrying the Time All One, weren't you? I expect it puts you especially in touch."

Eleni didn't believe a word of what she'd said. But Andreas, comforted, was now smiling broadly.

"Yes!" he said. "I reckon you're right. You know, it was like a voice inside me saying 'Pick up that pestle' and 'Hit him quick.' I don't suppose the Living God would normally speak to someone like me—just a priest's helper in a poor corner of the country—but with the Time All One there's no telling what might happen."

Reverently, he slipped the chain over his head and handed the medal to Eleni. "I must have been guided to borrow it from you," he said. "But it's yours. It was given to you, and you're the Messenger."

Eleni put on the chain and felt the medal settle against her chest. No, not exactly against her chest. She was still lean, but not quite as flat as she'd been when she became a fisherman, back in the spring. The medal was between her breasts.

It wasn't a welcome thought. Only the old woman so far had realized her sex. For a girl to wear male dress was so unthinkable in the islands that she hadn't otherwise been challenged. But could she go on getting away with it? She shuddered and pulled her tunic tight.

"Come along!" she said. "Let's be on our way!"

The stretch they were on turned out to be the last uphill stage. With the sun now above the horizon, they came over the top of the pass, and the world opened out before them.

None of them had ever seen such a sight. Below them, its outlines softened by early mist, lay a town that was many times larger than Molybdos village. It had docks and a harbor in which rode scores of ships, some of them great trading vessels. Morning sunshine glinted on an expanse of sea; beyond the sea, its outline still blurred and gray, was more land, rising to a plateau. Looking down at the closely packed rooftops, Nikos said, "This is Anatolis. Second-biggest city in the islands. We'll be pretty safe here. If those village oafs come looking for us, they'll never find us in a place this size. And at the other side, that's Chalcos, where we have to go next."

"Sooner the better, if you ask me," said Eleni.

"I've spotted the ferryboat," said Nikos. "There's two of them, one from each side of the strait. They've just crossed in the middle. They must go quite often. And I don't suppose anyone takes much notice of who's on them."

"We'll get the first one we can," Eleni said.

———

Her eyes had been following the movements of the ferry that was heading for Chalcos. Now she raised them, to look over to the land opposite. The spot where they were standing was higher than the bare upland plateau of Chalcos, and she could see its northern coastline receding into the distance. And beyond it—far away, yet not so far as it had been from Molybdos—the frail distant image of Mount Ayos could be seen, floating translucent in the sky.

"Hey, look at that!" she said to Andreas. "The mountain!"

Andreas's eyes lit up.

"The sign!" he cried. "Eleni, that *proves* you were right. It *was* the god's voice that spoke to me. I did what he wanted after all!"

· IX ·

THE TOWN BEGAN SUDDENLY. One minute Eleni, Andreas, and Nikos were trudging down the hillside; the next
they were among streets and surrounded by huddled
houses. Men drove donkeys or pushed carts. Street sellers
cried their wares. There were shops; Eleni had never in
her life seen a shop before. There were people who were
dressed in good cloth, and many more who looked as poor
as the villagers of Molybdos, but none who were dressed
quite like themselves. It was clear that here in Anatolis
their garb was outlandish. Yet nobody showed much interest in them, whereas on Molybdos any stranger would
be stared at, studied intently, and commented on. Once
a pair of riders went by on handsome horses. Eleni knew
they were horses, though she had never seen one before.
On their own steep island there were donkeys but no
horses.

They went down toward the quay, through a market-place crowded with people. Though they'd meant to find the ferry and leave Sideros at the earliest moment, they couldn't resist lingering and gazing wide-eyed at all the bustling activity. In a corner of the square a young man played a harp and another a flute, while a third sang plaintive songs; they listened for a while and Nikos said he didn't know the songs but his voice was better than the singer's.

And there were eating places. The smell of food reminded them that they'd only had one meal the previous day, and it had been a poor one. Suddenly they were all desperately hungry. But, never having paid for a meal, they didn't know what to do and were shy of entering. They were gathered in a little huddle in a narrow alley that led to the harbor, raising each other's courage to the point of going and ordering a meal, when Nikos grabbed the other two by their tunics and yelled, "Go back!"

Puzzled, but nervous and reacting swiftly, they darted back along the alley away from the quay. When they were around a couple of corners, Nikos halted.

"All right now," he said.

"Who was it, Niko?" Andreas asked. "That lot from the village? They can't be here already."

"No. Worse than that," said Nikos. "It's my father and Lukas, the lord's agent. They must have come by sea from Molybdos. They'll be looking for me." He grinned ruefully. "Or the money I took."

"We'd better get out of sight, then!" said Eleni, and she led them through the nearest open doorway. It was that of a tavern, and they found themselves going down stone steps into a warm, crowded basement.

"Well, Lukas and my dad won't come into a place like this!" said Nikos. And it was obvious even to them that it wasn't an establishment of high standing. The din was unceasing. Customers, who seemed to be mostly seamen, shouted, squabbled, and swore in loud, rough voices and accents they could hardly understand. Three or four servingmen pushed their way through the throng, shouting out orders for wine and food. Eleni, Andreas, and Nikos found themselves pinned against a wall, where they stood ignored for a while. Eventually one of the servers took notice of them and asked, "You want something? If you don't, that's the way out!"

"Food," said Eleni.

"Food? Over to that corner, then. Find room at a table." He hustled them through the crowd to a corner where there were a couple of long, rough wooden tables with benches. There didn't seem to be any room, but the servingman yelled, "Shove up!" to the occupants, who, barely stopping their eating and drinking, shuffled their backsides along the benches to let the newcomers in.

"Well, what do you want?" the man demanded.

"What have you got?"

"Same as they're all having. Stew. Bread and cheese. Both if you want."

"We'll have both!" said Nikos instantly, without wait-

99

ing for his companions' agreement. Eleni was too hungry to object.

The server shoved wine in front of them; this seemed to come without having to be ordered. It was a while before the stew appeared. Andreas asked, "Are you *sure* it was your father and Lukas, Niko?"

"It was them all right. Think I don't know my own father?"

"Maybe you shouldn't be dodging them, Niko," said Eleni. "It's your chance to go back home."

"And yours, too," said Nikos. "They could be looking for you as well. But if you think I'll tell them I've lost the money and then be hauled back to Molybdos by the scruff of the neck, you've another think coming."

"That fellow's listening, Niko," whispered Andreas. And indeed, two or three places along the table, a middle-aged man with a broad face and a graying beard was showing interest in them. When Eleni looked toward him he caught her eye and grinned.

The stew arrived and was vile. But it was hot food, and they weren't in a critical mood. They finished it and went on to the bread and cheese. Nikos drank a fair amount of the wine, which was rough and red, but Andreas and Eleni barely tasted it. Eleni had thoughtfully extracted three selenicas from her pouch, thinking this would be more than enough, but was startled when the servingman demanded nine.

"That's ridiculous," said Nikos. "Nine selenicas for what we've had!"

"You didn't have to have it. You should have asked the price first."

The three looked at each other in dismay. Nine selenicas would make a big hole in their wealth. They still had to pay the ferry and keep going until they got to Malama.

The customers who'd sat between Nikos and the bearded man had left by now, and the bearded man moved along the bench toward them.

"Come off it!" he told the server. "You can't get away with that. Thirty pennies each doesn't make nine selenicas!"

The servingman scowled.

"Because you pay thirty pennies, that doesn't mean everyone does," he said. "You're a regular, they're strangers. I can charge them what I like."

"Oh no, you can't. Not while I'm around." He turned to Eleni, who still had the three selenicas in her hand. "Give him just one of those, my dear. And tell him to bring you the change."

Eleni handed over the selenica. It didn't strike her until the server had reluctantly accepted it and hurried off in response to another order that the stranger had seen that she was a girl. The men in the village hadn't, but they weren't very observant.

"Are you going somewhere from here?" the stranger inquired.

"To Malama," said Nikos.

"Directly by sea, I suppose?"

"We don't think we can afford that," said Andreas.

———

"We were expecting to take the ferry to Chalcos and go overland."

"It's ten selenicas each for the passage from here to Malama," the stranger said.

"Then we definitely can't afford it. We'll *have* to go on foot across Chalcos."

"I wouldn't do that if I could help it. It's barren, you know. High and barren. Cold at night. Not many tracks, and they're easily lost. Stick to the seaways, every time, that's my advice. . . . I'd say from your speech that you come from the west somewhere, is that right?"

"Yes," said Andreas. "From Molybdos."

"Interesting. Molybdeans don't come this way much."

"Because they're too poor," said Eleni.

"May I ask why you're going to Malama, three young people on your own?"

Eleni and Andreas were instinctively reluctant to say anything about their mission. But Nikos, his tongue loosened by the wine, was willing to talk. Before long he was boasting about his singing voice and declaring his confidence that if once he got to Malama, he could soon win his way to fame and fortune.

Good voices were rare, the stranger agreed, and there were those in Malama who would appreciate them. He wished Nikos good luck. Had he misheard, or had there been some mention of Nikos's father? Did his father approve of this scheme?

Eleni gave Nikos a warning nudge in the ribs, but Nikos was talking excitedly. No, he said, his father was stuck in the mud of Molybdos and had no higher ambition for him than that he should get the job of steward in turn. Before long Nikos was telling the man he had just seen his father and the lord's agent, and they had obviously come to Anatolis in the hope of finding him and taking him home. He didn't say anything about the thirty gold helions he'd lost. But even without this information the stranger showed extreme interest in Nikos, and ordered more wine with which to ply him.

Andreas and Eleni said little. When Nikos presented them as merely a couple of friends he was taking along for company, they didn't trouble to contradict him. Once again, after a long night's walk, they were feeling sleepy.

"Well," said the stranger when he had learned all that Nikos could tell him, "it seems to me that with people looking for you it would be best to lie low until dark, and then get out of Anatolis as fast as you can. And I know a captain, an honest fellow and a good seaman, who'll be sailing for Malama on tomorrow morning's tide. He'll take you at a price you can afford. You can go on board tonight after dark. And until then, why don't you rest in my house? It's just across the little street at the back."

"How's *that* for an offer?" said Nikos to the other two. "Pretty good, eh?"

Andreas agreed with him. Eleni was more cautious by nature, and had some misgivings as they left the eating place in the stranger's company. Nikos peered both ways along the street with an elaborate show of caution, but there was no sign either of his father and the steward or of outraged villagers. The stranger's house was small and dark, but warm and comfortable.

"I'm a retired captain myself," he said. "Damis is my name, and I live alone. I like to have guests, especially young people. Now make yourselves at home while I go and arrange your passage with my friend."

"Well, we've fallen on our feet," said Nikos with satisfaction when Damis had gone.

"Seems like it," said Eleni. "If we can trust him."

"Why ever shouldn't we? He's a really nice helpful fellow. He saved us from being cheated, didn't he?"

"Yes, he did," Eleni said. "And he *seems* friendly. But . . ."

"I'm a pretty good judge of people," Nikos said. "I can tell just by looking at him that *he's* all right."

"He does seem nice enough," said Andreas, yawning. "And, after all . . ."

"After all, the Living God's looking after us, you mean," Eleni said dryly. "I think we should look after ourselves, all the same. Maybe we should go and find a ship for ourselves. Or even get away quickly, on the ferry."

"Are you crazy?" asked Nikos. "You'd run the risk of being caught, and of being cheated if we weren't caught, just because you can't bring yourself to trust *anyone*? Have a bit of sense, Eleni. As for me, I'm going to sleep."

Eleni looked across to Andreas in the hope of support, and realized that although he was sitting up he was glassy-eyed with sleep already. And she admitted to herself that the stranger had an open expression and an engaging manner. Also, she too was sleepy. In no time at all, Nikos was fast asleep on the bed and the other two on the sofa.

They were awakened by their new friend.

"Come along," he said cheerfully. "It's all arranged. Kaikos—that's my friend the captain—says he can remember being young and hard up himself. You'll pay him whatever you can afford. And you can go aboard right away. It's getting dark now, and there's a couple of crewmen waiting to take you to the ship."

When they reached the street, they found that in fact four people were waiting. Two of them were burly men in seaman's garb. The other two were surprising. They were a couple in filthy rags: a skinny man who stank of drink and stood up with the help of a grossly obese woman.

Eleni stared at them in horror. Damis noticed her reaction and said in a low voice, "Sorry about them. They're not the kind of company I'd have chosen for you. But Kaikos is a working captain, and can't afford to turn customers away."

Eleni muttered to Andreas, "I don't like this. Let's leave." But Andreas was looking at the dreadful couple with more pity than horror, while Nikos seemed amused. As they moved off toward the quay, Eleni realized that it wouldn't in fact be easy to break away: Damis and the two seamen were herding them.

They hadn't far to go. Almost at the nearest point on the quay, a small boat waited for them, lurking in the shadow of larger vessels. It drew alongside a flight of stone steps, and the ragged pair were maneuvered precariously aboard.

"Your turn now," said Damis.

Nikos went happily down the steps. But Eleni's doubts and fears rose rapidly to a conviction that this was a disaster. She grabbed Andreas's hand and hissed, "Andreas! Don't go!" He took a hesitant step toward her. And then they were both being forced down the steps by a suddenly ruthless Damis and one of the seamen. In almost no time they had been hauled aboard and the boat was nosing its way out from the quay. Damis stood on the steps and waved them good-bye. The smile on his face was one of mockery.

· X ·

THE DARK HULL of a ship loomed over them, and they were being forced by rough hands up a ladder to the deck of a cargo vessel, then down another ladder into its hold. Nikos protested loudly, demanding to know what was going on and proclaiming that he was a steward's son and this could not be done to him. The only results were a blow to the head from one seaman and a kick in the backside from another.

In the airless hold of the ship, lit by a single lamp, were about a score of people of both sexes. All looked poor and ragged. Several were drunk; others were curled up or propped up together, sleeping or trying to sleep. A woman held a thin, wailing child to herself. No one showed interest in the new arrivals or in Nikos's outburst, and their questions were met with blank stares and silences or incoherent mumbles.

Eleni could hardly prevent herself from complaining bitterly to Nikos, "*You* told us we could trust that fellow!" Then she looked at Andreas's miserable face, and held her tongue. Andreas had been trusting, too, and she didn't want to reproach Andreas.

From time to time through the night, hatches were raised and more bodies thrust into the hold. Most of those arriving seemed apathetic or bewildered, and there were more drunks. The hold became hot and crowded. The stink of stale wine and unwashed bodies grew stronger, and was made worse by smells of urine and excrement. Two or three buckets had been provided, and people jostled to use them. At length there were new arrivals who seemed to have some idea of what was happening, and the two words passed from mouth to mouth: "The mines!"

Eleni, Andreas, and Nikos huddled together in a corner. Even Nikos had fallen silent. Then, at one of the periodic openings of the hatch above, a voice bawled, "Nikos! Nikos of Molybdos!"

Nikos leaped to his feet. "That's me!"

"Come up here! Out of the way, you other lot!"

A man tried to force his way up the ladder, but was shoved back and fell on the floor. Nikos pushed through the throng and without a backward glance at his companions climbed up through the hatch, which closed behind him.

"Well!" said Andreas. "What do you think they want with him?"

Eleni had no idea. In the fetid air she was only just

conscious; thought had been driven from her mind. Hours went by and seemed endless. Sometimes, surprisingly, she and Andreas dozed. They didn't know whether it was day or night; down here it made no difference. Neither food nor water appeared. More people were thrust into the hold, and the crowding grew until there was no longer room to lie or even sit. The stench became worse and worse. From time to time Andreas's lips moved, and Eleni knew he was praying to the Living God. His prayers seemed to give him some comfort; he managed occasionally to smile and to press Eleni's hand.

At last the sounds of putting to sea were heard and the ship's motion felt.

"It can't be a long voyage," Andreas said, his voice now a croak. "They'd have had to give us water if they didn't want us all dead." And there was some slight encouragement in being under way. But before long the ship began to pitch and roll. In her time on board the *Seahawk* Eleni had never been seasick, but the confinement and foul air of the hold, added to the movement, were too much for her. She contained herself as long as she could, but in the end she had to throw up, and she was by no means the only person who did. Some people vomited over themselves; some over others. In a corner of the hold a fight broke out; somewhere else a woman cried wildly that her man was dead.

More time passed. The motion of the ship became smooth again; eventually the knocking and jarring of landing at a quay were heard. There was a long silence, except for the groans, snarls, and mutterings of the captives. At last the hatches were flung open, and a voice from above bawled, "Come on, now! Out of it!"

There was daylight above. Earlier there would have been a rush to the ladder, and skirmishing to get out first, but apathy and perhaps feebleness had set in. A few lethargic figures led the way, and the voice above had to shout, "There's water up here!" to give any vigor to the exodus. Even so, there wasn't much jostling. Stronger folk pushed weaker ones ahead of them; children were helped or carried up. The crowding down below grew gradually less. Eleni and Andreas, by silent agreement, hung back. Eleni had recovered the power of thought enough to begin wondering, and dreading, what might lie ahead.

At length they were the only people left, except for an unconscious man and a woman too weak to get up the ladder; no one, it appeared, had actually died. A burly seaman came down, apparently impervious to the filth and stench, slung each of the disabled pair in turn over a shoulder, and got them out of the hold. Eleni and Andreas were last of all.

There were buckets of water on the deck, from which they were allowed to drink. They dropped to their knees, cupped their hands, and had a moment's sheer joy from slaking their appalling thirst. Then, blinking in the light and slightly giddy, they were hustled across the deck and over a gangplank to the wharf.

Two or three other vessels were tied up, and there were a couple of single-story port buildings, but looming over them and dominating the landscape was a mountain. It was bare, bleak, gray-to-indigo in color, and without beauty. On its slopes, openings and the signs of workings could be seen; tracks led up and around its sides and carts were visibly moving. Lower down, between the mountain and the quay, was a shantytown, and a broad dirt road led to it from the harbor.

"We must be on Orichalcos," Andreas said. "Those are the orichalc mines up there. We've gone right past Chalcos itself."

On the quay the captives from the ship were straggling forward between a gauntlet of leather-jerkined soldiers who carried bludgeons. Each victim was roughly but thoroughly searched; a few coins and trinkets were removed, but there didn't seem to be much. At the front of the line a man in long tunic and fine cloth cloak inspected the prisoners, turning them around, prodding them, pinching arms and thighs, opening mouths, and sending them into one of three streams. One was of able-bodied men, a second of women and of older and less fit-looking men, a third of children and the obviously feeble or crippled. Beside the well-dressed man, another with a big leather pouch counted out money—a sum as each captive passed into one of the streams—to a man who appeared to be an officer of the ship. There were wails from children taken from their mothers, and protests from couples or companions who were separated. These were mostly ignored, though prisoners who showed signs of aggression got blows from the bludgeons. Eleni and Andreas, at the back of the line, looked at each other in horror. Eleni said, "This may be where *we're* split up."

Andreas's lips moved in prayer. As if in answer to the prayer, the seaman who'd called Nikos up from the hold appeared at his elbow.

"Here, you two!" he said. "Back to the ship! Captain wants to see you!"

The captain's cabin at the rear of the ship was poky, holding only a bunk, a table, and a bench. The captain, a thickset, swarthy, bearded man, sat at the table. There was hardly room for Eleni and Andreas to get inside, and the seaman withdrew to the door. The captain looked at them with some interest.

"You're the ones old Damis sent me," he said.

"Yes," said Eleni. "And there were three of us. What happened to our friend?"

"Your friend was bought out. Damis thought he would be. Get him on board, he said; his folk were around and they'd pay well for him. He was right; they did. He brought me more than he would have done here. Five times as much." The captain chuckled. Then he said, "They wouldn't pay for you two, though. Damis thought you might be worth something, but they weren't interested."

"Damis *sold* us, then," Andreas said.

"Yes. Of course he did. That's his business. He's one of our best suppliers. And he always tells me if he has merchandise that's a bit out of the ordinary. Has a good eye for an opportunity, Damis has."

"Merchandise!" said Andreas. "People are merchandise, are they?"

"No good sounding indignant, lad. Talk like that in the mines and you'll get lashes. Yes, most of what we handle is merchandise, no more, no less. And pretty worthless merchandise, mainly. Drunks and derelicts, ragged beggars, and so on. Might as well end their lives this way as any other."

"But the children?"

"What about them? There's work for children here. Work that children do best. And they're no-hope children, you know. Don't know who their parents are, or else they have useless parents. No prospects in life. But as for *you* . . ." He addressed Andreas. "What's your name, lad?"

"Andreas."

"That's right. A priest's helper, weren't you?"

Andreas nodded.

"That wouldn't save you from the mines. Not in itself, it wouldn't. Priests don't count for much, these days, and the mines need more and more bodies, with the King spending the way he does. But maybe you can read and write, or know a bit of healing?"

Andreas nodded again.

"Thought you might," said the captain. "I don't believe in wasting useful material. It's wicked to sell a person of talent for six or eight helions. Downright wicked. They might be worth twenty. As for *you* . . ." He turned to Eleni. "Say something."

"I could say plenty," said Eleni.

"That's enough. You don't *need* to say any more. I was just checking. Damis was right again. Said you weren't what you seemed, in more ways than one. A girl dressed as a boy, he said. And you are, aren't you? Now, just step into the light. Yes, Damis was right about that, too. Blue eyes. You know what blue eyes mean?"

"I've been told," said Eleni, remembering Hylas.

"They mean Gold Island, generally. But eyes and hair go together. Blue eyes, fair hair, that's aristocrats. Brown eyes, black hair, that's the rest of us. Blue eyes, black hair—well, I've heard tell of it, in a story when I was just a kid, about some hero or other, but I've never seen it in the Fortunate Isles before. So I reckon Damis was right and you're both special cases, maybe worth something. However, look after the pennies, they say, and the helions take care of themselves. Have you any money? If so, you can hand it over." He looked at Andreas. "You first."

"I've nothing," said Andreas. "See for yourself." He took off his tunic and passed it over the table. The captain felt it rapidly and passed it back. There was nowhere else on Andreas's meager person where money or valuables could have been hidden.

"What about you, dear?" he said to Eleni.

Eleni stared at him, sullenly.

"I'd hand over if I was you. Because if you don't I'll have you searched, and my sailors are rough men. You wouldn't like *them* searching you, I know."

Reluctantly, Eleni groped for her remaining money.

She thought of trying to keep some back, but the captain was watching her shrewdly.

"*All* of it, dear," he said. "I can always tell. . . . Thank you. Now, what's that round your neck?"

Eleni said, "I won't give you that, whatever you do."

"Let me just look at it. . . . Funny little thing. Is it worth anything?"

"Not to you it isn't," said Eleni.

"You're cheeky, aren't you? Don't forget, I could have you in the mines by just snapping my fingers. Still, I like a bit of spirit. And I daresay it's worth more to you than it is to me; it wouldn't fetch much. You can keep it, dear, with my compliments."

The captain grinned. "And I can read your mind. I know you're hating me, but I'll tell you now, you owe Damis and me a lot. There's many dealers and many captains that'd sell you to the mines as just a couple of bodies like the rest. You're lucky you came into *our* hands. You're not going into the mines; not at the moment, anyway. I'm going to show you to young Timokles. He's the assistant governor of Orichalcos, an aristocrat to his fingertips. We'll see what you're worth to him."

He called to the seaman, "Keep 'em under guard till Lord Timmi comes. He'll be here before long."

"Right you are, sir. We get them to clean up the shit?"

"Not on your life. Use some of the riffraff from the back of the queue. I want these two smelling sweet when His Nibs arrives. Give them water to wash in."

He turned to Eleni and Andreas, grinning.

"We'd better have you in a proper state for sale," he said. "Don't want him turning you down, do we? That wouldn't be in your interest or mine. You wouldn't like the alternative."

The tall young man with ash-blond hair arrived about midday. He slid lightly from his beautiful horse and threw the reins to an attendant. He strode across the quay and over the gangway, then recoiled at the stink still rising from the hold, from which came sounds of swabbing and slopping.

"Living God help us!" he said. "I'm not going near *that!*" He told a sailor, "Send the skipper ashore," and withdrew to land.

Eleni and Andreas were propelled ahead of the captain, who dropped a knee briefly to his superior.

"Well, how are you getting on, you old rogue?" the young man inquired. "Full load of bodies this time?"

"Pretty full, Lord Timmi. They get harder to find, though."

"I saw today's lot on their way to the mountain. There were some who looked as if they'd hardly make it, never mind do any work. The mine manager's been complaining to the governor. He says most of those we get these days don't last any time at all."

"Sorry about that," the captain said, "but we have to pick up what we can."

"I've told him so, but he doesn't understand. He thinks there's a bottomless pool of plebs. Doesn't realize we're down to the dregs."

"I've a couple of nice ones for you today, though," said the captain. "Specials."

Timokles cast an indifferent eye on Eleni and Andreas. "What's special about them?" he asked.

"Well, the boy's been a priest's helper. He can read and write."

"Oh? *Which* boy?"

"The one on the left. The other's a girl."

"Really?" Timokles sounded mildly surprised. "Let's see." He turned to Eleni. "Open your tunic."

Eleni, turning crimson, hugged it round her.

"Go on," the captain said. "Open up."

But the young man laughed. "All right," he said. "She needn't. The gesture tells me enough. And the creature has feelings. Interesting. You wouldn't be shy for long in the mines, girl. Once you get there, male or female, it's all just flesh. Now, you, the other one, the one who *is* a boy. You can read and write, you say?"

"Yes," said Andreas.

"Yes, *my lord!*" said the captain sharply.

"You're willing to be tested?" Timokles asked.

"Yes. My lord."

"I can't test you myself. Never went in for that kind of thing, there's too much else to do. But I've a man who'll test you. Thoroughly. And the Living God help you if I buy you and you can't perform. You'll be beaten to jelly and *then* sent to the mines. You understand?"

Andreas nodded.

"You can use a tablet and stylus?"

"Yes, my lord."

"Well," Timokles said, "there *is* a vacancy. We're short of tally clerks to check the ore and record deliveries. And the assayer's here from Malama; we need a clerk for him. You've timed it well, Captain. I might be interested, if the price was right. But why would I need the girl? I've as many girls as I want, and all of them prettier than this one."

"I stay with her, whatever happens," Andreas said.

"Quiet, you!" the captain told him. "You go where you're sent!"

But Timokles was amused. "Bravely spoken, creature," he said in an ironic tone.

"Look at her eyes, Lord Timmi!" urged the captain.

Timokles gazed into Eleni's face.

"Yes. I see. A half-caste. Somebody's been naughty somewhere. Well, that's happened before, but it doesn't usually work this way. When *we* mix with *them*, the brown eyes and dark hair get transmitted, not the blue and fair. And it's just as well. We don't have to ac-knowledge our little mistakes. But *blue* eyes in one of *them* . . . Yes, you rogue, she *is* special. I'd rather not send a girl with blue eyes to the mines. It wouldn't be decent."

He paused, then added thoughtfully, "All the same, she's not one of *us*. I might find her a job around the house. But you needn't think you can play on my con-science to get a high price. How much are you asking for these two?"

"Well, plebs that can write are scarce, Lord Timmi. I don't know how long it might be before we get another. I reckon the boy's worth thirty."

"Thirty selenicas, you mean?"

"Now, now, my lord. We're talking seriously, aren't we, not joking? Thirty helions."

"Rubbish. He's not worth half that."

"It's reasonable, Lord Timmi. You're paying for his training, remember. It takes time to teach a lad to read and write and do a bit of healing."

"*You* didn't pay for his training, you cheeky swine!"

"No, but I picked him out. You pay for my judgment."

"Twenty helions."

"No, my lord. I can't do it, even for you. I'm a poor man. Besides, my next trip's to Malama with a load of orichalc. I could sell him there instead. Prices are high in Malama. I'm only offering him to you because we're old friends, if you'll allow me to say so."

"Twenty-five, and that's final."

"Sorry, but I can't haggle. Tell you what, though, seeing it's you, just out of goodwill I'll knock a couple off. Twenty-eight."

"Twenty-seven."

"All right, my lord. Twenty-seven it is. Now, what about the girl?"

"She's not worth anything, really. If I buy her, it's sentiment. I'll give you ten."

"I'm soft hearted myself, my lord, but I can't afford to be *that* soft. Fifteen."

"I'll split the difference with you. Twelve."

"Tell you what, Lord Timmi. Twenty-seven and fifteen makes forty-two. You can have the pair of them for forty."

"Including shackles."

———

"Oh, all right. I've got a rusty old set knocking around somewhere. I'll throw them in free. Right you are, Lord Timmi, they're all yours."

Timokles beckoned to the attendant, who carried a leather pouch. "Pay him forty helions," he said, "and take them to the house. I must hurry now; I've royal company." To the captain Timokles said, "You've got the better of me again, you villain. I always finish by paying through the nose."

"No, Lord Timmi, you've drove a good bargain. You'll be well satisfied."

But as the young man strode away, the captain winked and said to Andreas, "Didn't know you were worth all that money, did you? Nor did I. He could have had you for twenty-five the pair. These aristocrats think they're clever, but we can run rings round them. Use your brains, you two; you'll come out all right and be thankful to me in the end."

A little later Andreas and Eleni, shackled together, were plodding along behind the attendant, who rode ahead of them at walking pace. Timokles had remounted and galloped away without a word or a backward look.

"Where are we going?" Andreas called to the attendant.

"To the Governor's house for now. After that, who knows? His lordship'll decide. At least it doesn't look like you're going up *there*."

He pointed to the mountain where the mines were. High, bare, and ugly, it dominated the landscape. Its slopes were gashed with black, irregular openings; there were abandoned roadways and tumbles of jagged stony debris. Flames from some outdoor operation could be seen; smoke drifted into the air and an occasional acrid whiff came to Eleni and Andreas. Lower down than the mine workings were the huddled shacks of the shanty-town. People, as small from this distance as insects, moved apparently at random over the sterile wastes. Nowhere on the entire mountainside was there a trace of green.

Eleni looked the other way, toward the sea. It was calm and lovely today, and on the horizon was another coast, which must be that of Gold Island. Somewhere in the same direction—distant still, but not so distant as it had been—was that other mountain: Mount Ayos, their goal. To glimpse in the east its clear, translucent outline would have cheered her spirit, but today it was not to be seen.

·XI·

Lord Timokles's servant led Andreas and Eleni around the side of the mountain toward a row of tall cypresses, which sheltered a large, elegant house from the unappealing sight of the orichalc mines. The house faced seaward, and from it a series of flower-planted terraces descended to the shore.

It was the most impressive dwelling that Andreas and Eleni had ever seen, far surpassing the steward's house on Molybdos. The servant's horse quickened its pace as it came within sight of home, and the chained pair could only just stumble along fast enough to stay upright. On the shadowed landward side of the house was a block of stabling and outbuildings. Andreas and Eleni, still shackled, were thrust into a small, dark, smelly shed and heard a locking bar rattle into place.

"Locked up again!" Eleni said. "I've had enough of this!"

Suddenly despair struck her, and with it came the impulse to take it out on Andreas. The quest was hopeless and it was all his fault. Here they were, shackled and shut away once more from the light of day. It was more than she could bear.

"You're crazy!" she told him. "Getting us into this! All that stuff about a Messenger! It's garbage. You hear? Garbage! I wish I'd never listened to you. I wish I'd never *seen* you. I wish you were dead. I wish *I* were dead! I only hope we soon will be!"

She broke into sobs: great, racking sobs that seemed to come from deep inside her. Andreas said nothing, but waited until the sobs began to die down. Then he tried to comfort her. She pushed him violently away, jerking the shackle against ankles that were already sore.

"I can't even get away from you!" she wailed.

Andreas said quietly, "Sit down, Eleni."

Sitting down wasn't easy, being shackled and in the dark. They managed to get themselves to the ground, propped with backs against the wall. Gradually Eleni's sobs diminished once more to sniffs and then to silence. For some time Andreas didn't venture to say anything. Finally he whispered, "Cheer up. We *do* have the Living God with us. Think of the signs we've had, and the Time All One. Think how we escaped from that village lockup, and how we were picked out for special treatment when we landed here. The god's looked after us so far, and he

123

won't let us down now. We know you've been called to go to him, and you'll get there in the end."

"So you say," muttered Eleni.

Andreas reached for her free hand with his own, and this time she didn't push him away. They sat in silence in the dark, stuffy place. Time passed. Now and again they dozed. Eleni said at last, "I think we shall die here."

"No, we shan't. We can't. Not till our mission's over." And then, aware that this argument didn't convince Eleni, Andreas added, "Lord Thingummy isn't going to waste forty helions on a couple of dead bodies."

That, at least, carried conviction. Eleni's spirit began to recover its normal resilience. "Sorry I was so awful," she said. "I guess we'll win in the end. Though I'd rather rely on *you* than that old god of yours!" She squeezed his hand. Shortly afterward the servant reappeared to lead them out into the fading evening light and across a court-yard from which they could glimpse, through an archway, a much grander, paved courtyard beyond.

The room to which they were now led lay between the two courtyards. It was the kitchen, and they knew it before they got there from the smells of roasting meat and new baking. Inside, it was warm. A great pot sat on a fire, and there were ovens, cooking utensils, hanging carcasses, great storage jars and bins. A stout, bustling middle-aged woman presided noisily over the scene, issuing orders to three or four minions. She looked up with interest as Eleni and Andreas hobbled in.

"So *them's* what his young lordship's been buying," she said. "Let's have a look. . . . What did he pay for them?"

"Forty helions the pair."

"Forty helions! What it is to be rich, and have the governor as your uncle! Still, a fool and his money are soon parted. They don't look worth much to me."

"They're a boy and a girl. The boy can write, or so he says."

"H'm. I suppose you have to pay for that. I wish *I* could. . . . And the girl, if that's what she is? What's special about her?"

"*I* don't know, Kleo. Maybe he fancies her. She has blue eyes, didn't you notice? These lords are keen on blue eyes."

"Blue eyes and fair hair is what lords like," the cook said, "and the fairer the better. This one's hair's like the underside of a cooking pot. Black as soot. *She's* not Lord Timmi's type, I can tell you. He likes them fresh and blond and curvy, and straight out from Gold Island. And gets them, too. What would he want *her* for?"

"Listen, Kleo, I'm only the servant. He doesn't tell me what he's up to. He told me to bring them here and I've brought them."

"And I suppose they'll have to be fed?"

"Yes, please!" said Eleni.

"You be quiet," said the cook. "It's nothing to do with you."

"Of course they'll have to eat. He bought them; he'll want them kept in good condition. And I don't suppose they got much on that ship. You're not short of food, are you?"

"It's just as well I'm not. More mouths to feed, without

any notice!" Then the cook went on, in a tone that mixed contempt with rough kindness, "All right, you two, get some of this inside you." She gave them hunks of bread and generous bowls of stew and cups of wine-and-water, and when they'd gobbled the stew she refilled the bowls without a word.

"Now what?" the cook asked when they had finished.

"The boy's to be tested, to see if he can really write. The Living God help him if he can't! I expect old Pamphilos will send for him. Apart from that, we just wait for orders. Maybe I'll put them back in the shed."

"I wouldn't put a dog in there. Leave 'em with me, Glaukos. They can't go far, hobbled. I'll keep an eye on them. You hear that, you two? You just stay in this kitchen and be thankful I'm kindhearted. Any noise or trouble, and you'll regret it!"

Eleni and Andreas didn't have to wait long in the kitchen. A boy came to take them to the counting house, where Pamphilos—a long, thin, lugubrious-looking man—was making rapid calculations on his fingers, noting down the results from time to time on a wax tablet. At first he took no notice of the newcomers, but after a while he thrust a tablet and stylus at Andreas and said, "Take this down." He reeled off details of household supplies in a swift, monotonous voice. Andreas, who was out of practice, was soon struggling, and at one point had to admit that he was falling behind. Pamphilos frowned, but gave him time, and when he'd finished held out his hand for the tablet. He scrutinized it.

"Not bad," he said. "You'll have to write smaller than that, though. Can't take a cartload of tablets to the mines. Now, erase and try again."

Andreas smoothed out his writing with the flat end of the stylus and took fresh dictation. Gaining confidence, he worked faster and more neatly. Eleni watched with admiration; she'd never seen writing in progress before. Pamphilos examined the result and said to Andreas, "You'll do. In fact, compared with some of the clots that get clerking jobs here, you're good. I'll tell his lordship so. He'll be glad. It's what he wants to hear. Now, just you wait here until he's ready to see you."

Eleni and Andreas had no choice but to wait, for they were still shackled together. But once again they didn't have to wait long. Lord Timokles's servant reappeared and led them along a passage and into a great chamber that was obviously the principal reception room of the house. To Eleni it seemed splendid, for the whole floor area was tiled in mosaic, and there were paintings and tapestries on the walls. At one end was a hearth, with a log fire burning; at the other end was a small shrine to the Living God. Andreas automatically made the gesture of homage.

Four men lay propped on couches that were drawn up in a half circle. One was Lord Timokles, who held in his hand the tablet on which Andreas had been writing. The second man, toward the middle, was elderly, heavily built, bearded, and almost bald; the third was stocky, a little older than Timokles, fair and clean-shaven. He wore, like the others, a tunic of fine linen, though he didn't have quite the air of aristocratic ease that marked his companions.

But it was the fourth man whose appearance made Eleni gasp in astonishment. It was Prince Hylas—a little older, thinner in face and more serious-looking than when Eleni had seen him last, but still handsome and golden. His hound lay dozing beside his couch. Hylas glanced without great interest at the two figures in front of him, plainly not recognizing Eleni, but said in a tone of mild surprise, "Shackles!"

"You don't like them, Hylas, do you?" Timokles said.

"Neither do I. Not in the house, anyway." He turned to his servant. "Glaukos, have those things taken off. We're not having anyone shackled in this room."

Glaukos went out. Timokles passed the tablet to the older man.

"Nice neat writing, eh, Uncle?" he said.

"My dear Timmi, don't trouble me with these things. It's Myiskus's affair. He's the one who has to be satisfied." He handed the tablet on to the stocky man, who looked at it with professional interest, studied Andreas shrewdly, and asked, "Can you do numbers?"

"A bit."

"Add? Subtract? Multiply?"

"Well, I'm out of practice, sir, but I used to."

"What's four and eight?"

"Twelve."

"Fifteen, take away five?"

"Ten."

"Six times seven?"

Andreas hesitated a moment, then said, "Forty-two."

Timokles said to the older man, "Pretty good, eh, Uncle? And all done in his head. I reckon I got a good bargain."

The older man grunted.

Myiskus said, "He'll do for me, Governor. It's only for two or three days, anyway. It doesn't worry me that he hasn't experience of the mines. I don't like my clerk and the overseers to know each other. Too much scope for cheating."

Glaukos came back, accompanied by a servant who removed the shackles from Eleni and Andreas. Hylas remarked, "Their ankles are sore."

"So they are," said Timokles. "Shackles do that. It can't be helped."

Hylas asked, "Do you have an ointment for that kind of thing?"

"My dear Hylas," Timokles protested, "what's come over you since you were in the war? Such concern for the plebs?"

"I suppose they're human," said Hylas. "Like us."

"Not *quite* like us, I hope."

The old man said, "I had these feelings, once. You get hardened, Hylas, I'm afraid. If we treated the plebs like our friends and relations, we'd never get orichalc out of the mines at all. All the same, if it's distressing you . . ." He turned to Glaukos and said, "Tell the housekeeper to send us some stuff for sores." And to Timokles he said, "What about the girl? What's *she* doing here?"

"She was part of the deal," Timokles said.

"Do we have a use for her?"

"I thought we might find one. Helping in the house, perhaps. I don't like the thought of sending her to the mines. I told you—do you remember?—she has blue eyes. You can't see them well in this light, but they're blue all right, *our* blue."

Hylas said musingly, "Blue eyes, dark hair. That reminds me . . ."

The Governor said, "Timmi, I've seen a great deal in my time, and I'll give you a warning. Never encourage half-castes. They do get produced from time to time, human nature being what it is, but they're supposed to be destroyed at birth, and so they should be. We have to keep ourselves distinct from *them*. Now I know a few half-castes slip through the net and grow up, but as they're nearly always dark they get regarded as ordinary plebs and there's no harm done. A blue-eyed half-caste's a rarity, no doubt about it, but she's still a half-caste, and best out of the way. Don't treat her as special, my boy. Send her to the mines and be done with it."

Hylas said, "I must say, Governor, I feel the same way as Timmi, I don't quite know why. There *is* something special about blue eyes and black hair. I mean, there are thousands of *us* and tens of thousands of *them*, but I've only once before seen the blue-black combination, and that was a few months ago, a long way from here. It was a girl, and I *did* feel she was exceptional—marked out in some way. I've thought about her from time to time ever since."

Eleni couldn't contain herself any longer. She burst out, "Lord Hylas, it was me! Eleni from Molybdos! Your dog went for my goat, remember? You gave me a gold coin."

Hylas got up swiftly from his couch. He strode over to Eleni and put his hands on her shoulders.

"Look at me!" he said; then, "Yes. You're the one all right. Eleni from Molybdos. How in the Living God's name do you come to be here?"

"We were on our way to Gold Island . . ." Eleni began. Hylas interrupted her.

"Yes, of course! I suggested you should, didn't I? I said we might meet again, and we have! But how extraordinary. What happened?"

"They were picked up as vagrants and shipped to the mines," Timokles said. "Or rather, they'd have been in the mines if I hadn't bought them. You mean you actually *know* this creature, Hylas? I can hardly believe it."

"It's true," Hylas said. "I'm glad you found them."

"Then I feel quite pleased with my property."

"I'm *not* your property," Eleni declared indignantly. "You've *got* me but you don't *own* me. I'm *mine!* And whatever happens, me and Andreas are together!"

The Governor looked baffled. "This is getting beyond me!" he said. "I'm not used to hearing plebs carry on like this. And I'm tired. I want to go to bed. I shall leave you young men to your own devices. Hylas, you're the King's son and it's not for me to tell you how to behave, but I do beg you, don't encourage impertinence. . . . Now, what about tomorrow? You're only here for a few days, I know, while Myiskus does his assaying. Would a spot of hunting appeal to you?"

"Not tomorrow, Governor. You remember, I came with Myiskus so I could see for myself what goes on in the mines."

"A dreary way to spend a day! Oh well, please yourself, Hylas. We'll hunt the day after, eh? Good night."

He made his way, heavily, from the room. Hylas, Timokles, and Myiskus wished him good night. Myiskus said, "There'll be a lot of writing for Andreas to do tomorrow. That means taking a bag of tablets. I need someone to carry them."

"I don't mind doing that," Eleni said, "so long as I'm with Andreas."

Hylas laughed heartily.

"There you are, Timmi!" he said. "She doesn't see it as impertinence. She'll do us a favor—if she feels like it. Anyone would think she was a princess. You'll enjoy having her around the house, I can see. A servant with a mind of her own."

"I'm not sure that's what I require of my servants," said Timokles doubtfully.

Glaukos came in with a pot of ointment. Andreas took it from him and began applying it to Eleni's ankle.

Glaukos asked, "What's to be done with them tonight? Are they to be shackled again, my lord?"

Timokles said to Eleni and Andreas, "You've enough sense to know you're in luck. And you can't get off the island. If you ran away, you'd soon be caught, and you know what that would mean. I shall leave you unshackled." To Glaukos he said, "That's the decision. They can sleep in the servants' quarters. And tell Cook they're to be up at dawn, breakfasted and ready to go to the mines. With us."

·XII·

THE KITCHEN WAS CLOSING down for the night. In the warmest, most comfortable corner lay the cook, asleep and snoring already. One by one the nine or ten other servants lay down, in such clothing as they wore, in positions that were clearly well established by strength or seniority. Andreas and Eleni, as newcomers, found themselves in the one vacant space, against the wall that was farthest from the fire. Glaukos, directing them roughly to lie down and keep quiet, whispered to them to be thankful that they weren't fettered.

"But don't let it go to your heads," he added. "And now, get some sleep. You've a long day coming up tomorrow."

Eleni was no longer too shy to lie twined with Andreas. His steadiness and affection were her comfort. She put her arms around him simply and naturally. But her thoughts were on Hylas, on the astonishing and barely believable facts that he was here, had recognized her, and had spoken kindly to her. Was it possible that he would actually help her to get to Gold Island? It seemed at the moment that she was to be a house servant and Andreas a clerk, but that was almost equally incredible. She lay awake, long after Andreas was asleep and the kitchen was filled with the sounds of heavy breathing from all corners, topped by the noisy rise and fall of the cook's snores. Then, suddenly, it was morning, and she'd slept after all, and she and Andreas were being kicked into life by Glaukos.

The kitchen was still dark, but servants were stretching and yawning; there were lamps lit, and the cook, up and about already, was stirring one of her great pots.

"Grab a bowl and get some of that," Glaukos directed them. The cook ladled out a thick, gluey substance that tasted of nothing in particular but lined their stomachs. Then they were out in the cool before-dawn air. The stable block, in the range of buildings opposite the kitchen, was busy already; they could hear, coming from inside it, raised voices and the whinnying of horses.

"Mounts for the nobles," said Glaukos. "But we have to go ahead of them in *this* thing." In the yard a mule cart and driver waited. Andreas and Eleni climbed into the clumsy vehicle; Glaukos sat behind them and called an instruction to the driver.

The sky was lightening in the east; the shapes of build-

135

ings and the outlines of trees began to emerge. The mule cart moved easily down the driveway that led from the governor's house, then lurched its way along a rough road toward the shantytown. And here it came up behind the tail of a great, loose procession, twenty people wide and many scores deep, that was making its way up the hillside. At the front of it several of the leaders carried flaring torches, but at a shouted command these were put out, for there was light enough now for the procession to see where it was going. Around its margins, harrying and hurrying it along, ranged guards with long whips, which they applied to the backs of stragglers. The stragglers were mostly old men, women, and children.

"Going to work," explained Glaukos casually. He grinned. "You might have been among them yourselves," he said. "You've fallen on your feet, I can tell you. Thank your stars and the Living God."

Andreas made the gesture of homage, but Eleni thought deep, troubling thoughts, and was silent.

The mule cart turned off from the broad trodden way up which the mass of people were trudging, and followed a rising track that wound around the side of the mountain. The driver halted his cart at the entrance to a dark, narrow tunnel, where a group of three men in light-colored cloaks stood talking together. At a respectful distance from them was a cluster of underlings in the coarse tunics of the people. Glaukos got down from the cart, approached the nearest of the group of three, pointed to Andreas and Eleni, and said, "Assayer's assistants, sir. The nobles and the assayer are on their way."

The man, middle-aged and authoritative-looking, merely nodded.

"They said they'd be here by dawn," one of his companions observed. "But I suppose dawn means something different for nobles. And still more for princes. Have you met Prince Hylas before?"

"No," said the first man. "He never showed interest in the mines before. None of the royal family ever do. They'd rather not know where all the wealth comes from. But Hylas has changed, they say. He's poking his nose into all kinds of things that aren't really his business."

"He doesn't have to see *everything*, surely?"

"Apparently he does. And by going round with the assayer, he *will* see everything; that's what the assayer's for. There isn't much we can conceal anyway. He'll just have to understand that this is how we work."

"It all sounds rather a bore," said the third man.

"I merely hope he'll come soon," said the first. "I have better things to do than hang about all day."

It was full light now; the day was fine but not yet warm. Those in the group of underlings, with whom Eleni and Andreas now stood, hugged themselves and stamped their feet; the three cloaked men fidgeted impatiently and passed a leather bottle between them. At last three figures on horseback could be seen approaching. Men stepped forward from the group to take their horses as they dismounted: Prince Hylas, Lord Timokles, and the assayer, Myiskus.

The men in cloaks were introduced as the management of the mines.

———

"We shall take you in through this side shaft, Prince Hylas," the first of them explained. "It leads us straight to the work face. Then you can follow the process all the way through."

Torches were lit, and the men who carried them led the way into the dark, narrow tunnel. Before they entered it, the assayer looked around for Andreas and Eleni, and beckoned to them to fall in behind him. Glaukos waved them a farewell. "*I* don't have to go in there," he said, "the Living God be thanked."

The tunnel wound slowly downward. The air grew warmer as they went. Sounds could be heard from somewhere ahead of them: mostly the smiting sound of metal on rock, but sometimes a rumble as of falling debris, and occasionally shouts and cries. Then the passage opened out, and they were in a wide area, like a large underground cave, its roof propped by great wooden pillars. It was hot with the heat of human bodies, and there was a smell of sweat. A dozen men, totally naked, hewed with pickaxes at a rock face; in the flickering light—which came mostly from lamps strapped to their foreheads—their bodies seemed to change color from moment to moment. Behind them a bearded fellow in a loincloth strode back and forth, shouting at them in some guttural, incomprehensible language. One man who relaxed for a moment was lashed across his back, which showed the marks of many lashes already.

The seam they were working could be distinguished from the rock above and below by its red-gold metallic shine. Myiskus beckoned Andreas to him.

"There you are," he said. "That's the crude orichalc. We'll be following it through."

Small children, intent on their work and ignoring the visitors, were worming their way through to the work face, gathering up lumps of rock that the pickmen had hewed and carrying them away through other tunnels. More sounds of hewing and rockfall could be heard from beyond the cavern, and the party went through a tunnel to another face and then to another. At one of these faces the toilers had a brief break while an overseer, in the loincloth that seemed the sign of authority, marked the rock to show how it should be cut; at another there was a pause while props were brought in to shore up the roof. Apart from these short breaks, the rock faces were worked incessantly by the naked, sweating men under threat of the lash.

"The guards are barbarians from the mainland," the assayer told Andreas in an aside. "They can't understand the workers and the workers can't understand them, so there's no chance of ganging up."

Eleni and Andreas soon lost their bearings in the maze of interlocking caverns and tunnels. The heat was oppressive; their throats were choked with dust and their heads ached with the ring of picks on rock. Timokles was lagging behind the party, following it with increasingly obvious boredom and reluctance; Hylas's face, when it could be seen in the uncertain light, was grim, but he stalked determinedly on and seemed to be pressing the managers to be shown even more.

Eventually the party turned along a broad tunnel, lit all

the way by lamps, which led to the open air. Eleni and Andreas took deep, thankful breaths. Outside, the day was now fairly warm. From the main tunnel and others, the naked children converged with their burdens of rock, set them down on the flat ground outside, and were sent instantly back at a trot into the mine. Women and older men picked up the fragments of rock and pounded them in huge stone mortars with iron pestles until they were reduced to tiny bits and pieces; others then took the little stones and ground them to powder in big, heavy hand mills. Some of these workers had a few rags of clothing; others were naked. All alike were lashed or cudgeled if they showed signs of flagging.

Women now washed the powder in broad pans, in which the glistening orichalc sank to the bottom. Others, closely watched by guards, took this residue away, weighed it, and mixed it with measured amounts of some catalyst before putting it in sealed pots and into one of a row of furnaces.

"And after seven days," said the mine manager, "you see what we have." He went to a furnace that had cooled and told an overseer to draw out a pot, unseal it, and show the visitors what was inside. Even the nobles gasped to see it, for it shone with the red-gold fire of refined orichalc.

Timokles, in the tones of one anxious to get away, said, "Thank you, Manager. Most enlightening. I see you have everything under control." But Hylas, contemplating the precious metal and the scores of men, women and children who labored with pestles, mills, and furnaces on the hillside, said thoughtfully, "And all this goes to my father."

"Of course, Prince Hylas," the manager said. "Three cartloads a week go down to the harbor for shipment to Malama. And, if I may be forgiven for boasting a little, we are producing more now than was ever produced before."

"With the aid of barbarians wielding whips."

"It's not a pretty sight, Prince, I admit. But it's the only way we can get results. The creatures who work here are the dregs. Take off the whips and they'd just lie around doing nothing."

"Some of them look ready to drop dead."

"It's no problem if they do, Prince. We soon clear them out of the way. There's a burial trench round the side. We do need replacements, though. If you and Lord Timokles could indicate to the governor that an increased supply would be welcome . . ."

"More bodies, more output, you mean?"

"Precisely."

"And to think," said Hylas, half to himself, "that the result of all this toil is spent by my father to buy bloodshed in distant countries!"

"Hylas!" said Timokles sharply. "Should you . . . ?"

"No, of course I shouldn't say such things!" said Hylas. "The King can do no wrong. Though from what I hear, it seems the Living God may not care for his adventures. . . ."

"*Sssssh!* You'll be overheard!"

141

"And that would never do," said Hylas. He turned to the mine manager. "Thank you very much," he said formally. "I am impressed by your achievements. Naturally I shall inform the King."

There was a wary look on the manager's face. It was possible that Hylas's dry tone didn't escape him. But he took a formal farewell of the two nobles. Glaukos had brought their horses, and they rode away.

Hylas didn't look around. It was plain to Eleni that he hadn't even noticed her this morning. Well, she thought, that wasn't a surprise. He had other things on his mind, and she'd wager they were the same things as were on hers. If *she* were the king's son or had access to the Living God, they'd be getting an earful about the poor devils in there. . . .

"Now," said the assayer, "I can get some work done. I want to take a good look at one of those faces. Seems to me it isn't marked out right, and maybe it shouldn't be worked at all. Come along, Andreas. And you, too, Blue-eyes. We can't all be noble sightseers. Some of us have to earn a living."

In the next three days Andreas and Eleni worked hard. The first day was the worst, for it was all spent in the depths of the mine, as Myiskus examined the various orichalc seams and made calculations of comparative richness and workability. The heat made him tetchy; he had a couple of altercations with overseers and a dispute with one of the under managers. Twice he bawled Andreas out for slowness in getting down the details he dictated; once he complained of error but found the error was his own. Eleni, carrying his instruments and the bag of tablets, had an easier passage, with the doubtful advantage that she had time to observe the brutalities and miseries that surrounded her. The barbarian guards were aware that she wasn't one of the wretches in their charge; they scowled when she went past but never touched her with their whips, and this gave her a guilty sense of privilege. The sight of so many naked men and women, driven beyond all hope of modesty or care for privacy, affronted her deeply and made her uneasy in her own safely covered body.

Once Eleni recognized a Molybdos man, one of those who'd volunteered for the war. He was haggard and ill-looking now, with tangled hair and stubbly cheeks.

"Dio!" she greeted him. "Dio! Don't you know me? It's Eleni. Eleni, from Molybdos!"

The man turned aside for a moment from the work face at which he was hewing. She hadn't any doubt who he was, but he looked at her dully, with no sign of recognition. An overseer came along the line, and without saying a word the man resumed work. It was one of many bad moments. At the end of the day, when the mule cart took her and Andreas back to the Governor's house, Eleni was sick, retching, headachy, and unable to touch the rough but nourishing food the cook would have given her.

On the second and third days they were at least out of doors while Myiskus carried out tests on the ore-bearing rock, the various processes applied to it, and the orichalc that finally emerged. Halfway through the afternoon of the third day, he pronounced his task complete, and sent for his horse and for the mule cart.

"Hylas and Timokles are on Chalcos today, hunting," he told Andreas as they waited. "They'll be back tonight. The royal ship will be here to pick us up, with Princess Hermione and the Lady Phoebe on board. Tomorrow, all being well, we'll sail for Malama. And Andreas, if I can do a deal with Timmi, I want to take you with me. I could use you as my permanent clerk. How'd you like that?"

Andreas said, "I thought you weren't pleased with me. You kept bawling me out."

"Oh, that's just my way. You'll have to get used to it. My bark's worse than my bite. Actually, you're the best clerk I've ever had, and I don't want to lose you."

"But . . . what about Eleni?"

"Her? Where does she come into it? I don't need her. Anyone can carry a bag."

"We're together. I won't go anywhere without her."

"Don't be absurd, lad. Don't throw up your chances for a girl. A skinny creature like her, too. I won't hear of you not coming."

Eleni said, though her heart sank, "Go on, Andreas. He's right. You'd better go."

"I won't."

Suddenly Myiskus was furious. "All right, then," he snapped. "I'll take you at your word. You're not coming. I've given you your chance, and you've thrown it up. You aren't all *that* marvelous, you know. There's lots of clerks in Malama. You can go to the underworld for all I care. Good-bye!"

An attendant arrived with his horse, and he rode off. Soon afterward the mule cart came for Andreas and Eleni. As it trundled on its way, Eleni said, "Why can't you have a bit of sense and look after yourself?"

Andreas said, "I know what I'm doing. I know in the end you'll see the Living God, because the prophecy says so. If I stick with you, I can't go wrong. Besides, I'm your friend."

Eleni said, "You're as daft as a pumpkin. But I like you like that."

Andreas reached for her hand and she let him take it. She wondered whether Hylas was back from hunting.

·XIII·

THERE WAS A DISPUTE in the kitchen after supper. The cook told Andreas to bring in logs for the fire. Andreas would have done so, but Eleni intervened on his behalf and said he'd done a day's work already. Anyway, she said, he worked for the assayer, not for the cook. Andreas said he didn't work for the assayer anymore, and he didn't *mind* fetching logs. Eleni told him crossly to stand up for himself. The cook told Eleni to mind her own business. Eleni said she would gladly bring in logs herself but she wouldn't have Andreas pushed around. The cook said that if Eleni didn't behave herself she'd get a whipping. Eleni challenged her to try it.

Andreas said, "Eleni, I know why you're in a state. It's because of the poor sods in the mine, isn't it? But having a row with Cook doesn't do anything for them. She's not responsible."

Eleni, suddenly deflated, apologized comparatively meekly to the cook, and she and Andreas went to fetch logs.

They had just finished this task when Glaukos came in to say that the two of them were to go in and see the nobles at once. They stared at each other, then followed him to the great chamber they'd been in previously. The three young men were there, but not the Governor. Hylas and Timokles were recounting to Myiskus the story of a wild boar that had got away. Hylas's hound lay at his feet, and he bent down to stroke its head from time to time.

Myiskus looked up as Eleni and Andreas came in. He grinned. "I told you, Andreas, my bark's worse than my bite. You haven't missed your chance, not really, though you damned nearly did. You can still come with me to Malama, and I hope you will."

Andreas said, "I haven't changed my mind. I don't go anywhere without Eleni."

Myiskus said to the two nobles, still grinning, "You hear? He's as proud as you are, and a good deal prouder than me." And, turning to Andreas, he added, "Thanks to Prince Hylas, you may get your way."

"What do you mean?"

"I may have a job for Eleni," Hylas said casually. "My little sister's been saying for a long time she should have her own personal maid. How would you like to be a lady's maid, Eleni?"

Eleni was too startled to speak.

Hylas laughed at her expression. "Takes you by surprise, doesn't it?" he said.

"B-but what does a lady's maid *do*?"

"That depends on the lady. The maid does what she tells her. Light work, not scrubbing floors. Helping her dress and looking after her clothes and . . . well, making herself useful, I suppose." Hylas's voice trailed vaguely away.

"I've never been trained for that kind of thing."

"You're intelligent, you'll soon learn." Then, with mild irritation, "The Living God knows, it's hard work trying to help you people! You resist all the way!"

"What if your sister doesn't like me?"

"Then I suppose you won't last long. But at least you'll get to Malama, and you can look for work there."

Timokles said, "Hold on. Not so fast. Don't I have a say in this? These two belong to me. I paid good money for them."

"How much?" the assayer asked.

"Forty helions, to a ship's captain."

"He saw you coming. It's an absurd price."

"Maybe. But you and Hylas seem to want them. And, for that matter, I haven't lost interest in them myself. I don't see why I should give them away."

"How do the forty helions divide?"

"Twenty-eight for the boy, twelve for the girl."

Myiskus's face fell.

"Outside my range," he said. "Sorry, Andreas. I didn't realize you were in that price bracket. I can't afford you."

Hylas said, casually, "*I* can afford them. My father keeps me fairly well supplied. Though having seen where his wealth comes from, I feel a bit guilty about it. *I'll* give you your forty helions, Timmi."

"I'm not sure that I want to part with them."

"I might even give you fifty."

"Oh, come now, Hylas. I'm not a trader. I don't make a profit off my friends. Look, if you really want them you can have them for what I paid. I'll expect a favor from you sometime, in return."

"All right, that's a deal. My man will give you the forty."

The assayer said, "But Hylas, that doesn't solve the problem. You don't want Andreas, do you? I do, but I'm a poor man. I can't pay you twenty-eight for him, or anything like it."

"I'll lend him to you. He's my property, but you can have him on permanent loan. The condition is, you give him time off occasionally to see Eleni. You live on the Inner Ring, after all—just around the corner from the Palace."

"Hylas," said Timokles, "you're a sentimental idiot. You're doing all this because you find these two creatures' devotion touching. And the way you carried on last night about conditions in the mines was nearly giving my uncle an apoplectic fit. I don't know what's come over you. All this concern for the riffraff. It used to be hunting and horse racing, girls and gaming. Now you've gone so deadly serious I hardly know you anymore."

"It's right that princes should be serious," said the assayer primly. "Princes have responsibilities."

———

"If you'd said that to him last year," said Timokles, "he'd have rolled on the floor laughing. As for buying a couple of slaves out of sheer softheartedness . . ." Then it seemed that a thought struck him, and he went on slyly, "Unless, of course, he *fancies* the girl. I can't say skinny dark ones appeal to *me*, but some of us have bizarre tastes."

Hylas said amiably, "If you're not careful, Timmi, I shall knock you down. Look, you've made the poor creature blush. Can't I buy a present for my little sister without having to listen to your remarks?"

He turned to Andreas and Eleni.

"You're my property now," he said, "if you'll allow me to use that phrase. Off you go and get some sleep, and be ready at dawn. We're sailing for Malama."

Eleni woke before dawn, her stomach fluttering with mingled excitement and apprehension. Andreas, beside her, was awake already. His lips were moving, and Eleni knew he was giving thanks to the Living God for helping them on their way. Not for the first time, she half believed that this must be happening. Then she returned to her usual frame of mind. It was chance, and chance had favored them so far. And she was getting the adventure she'd craved. Perhaps she was getting too much of it. . . .

She wondered, for the first time in days, how Anasta was getting on without her, and what her brother, Milos, might be up to. She had a sudden yearning to see them and her home again. She wondered, too, whether Nikos had arrived back in Molybdos, and if so what he might have told the people there. And then she dozed off, and was being awakened, gently, by Andreas; opening her eyes, she was surprised by an expression of tenderness on his face that she hadn't expected. But as soon as he knew she was looking at him, it was suppressed.

Outside, the mule cart was waiting. On board were Glaukos, with the assayer's instruments and tablets, and Hylas's manservant, who held the hound on a lead. Eleni knew the man at once, from their encounter on Molybdos, but he showed no sign of recognizing her. And he had a message for her, delivered without apparent interest: She was to stay and wait for the Prince.

The cart trundled away and Eleni was left behind, wondering uneasily if something had gone wrong and she was to be separated from Andreas after all. Time passed. The sky lightened, and she looked with loathing at the bleak outline of the mountain from which the orichalc was quarried at such human cost. Then there were voices, the whinnying of horses, and the jingling of harness from the direction of the stables, and Hylas was calling "Eleni! Here!" She found herself being hoisted onto the back of a horse, and Hylas was mounting it in front of her and telling her to hold on tight, and in panic from the unaccustomed movement she was gripping him around the waist. He shouted to her over his shoulder, "Can't have a lady's maid arriving in a muck cart." And he was spurring the horse to catch up with Timokles and Myiskus, who had gone ahead.

Close to her eyes was the back of Hylas's head, with the blond hair floating lightly from it; in her arms was his torso, all hardness and muscle. The motion of the horse beneath her was strangely disturbing; she was at once excited and deeply embarrassed.

The journey that had seemed long when she and Andreas hobbled in fetters was short enough on horseback. Soon she was at the quay, where the beautiful ship that had brought Prince Hylas to Molybdos was moored. A gangway had been lowered, and the gear from the mule cart carried on board. The nobles and the assayer dismounted; Hylas swung Eleni easily to the ground and grinned into her still-embarrassed face. Attendants took charge of the horses. And then a girl came running down the gangway from the ship.

She was a little older than Eleni, light boned and delicately made, and she was the strangest and prettiest creature Eleni had ever seen. Her hair was a pale, pale blond, and braided down her back; her complexion suggested wild rose or apple blossom; her eyes were harebell-blue. She wore a butter-yellow gown, pinned over each shoulder, drawn in by a sash at a tiny waist, and allowing a glimpse of slender ankles and sandaled feet. She seemed so light that she barely touched the ground. Eleni, who never thought from one month to the next of her own appearance, suddenly felt coarse and ugly.

The girl ran to Hylas, reached up, and threw her arms around his neck. Hylas smiled down and kissed her.

"Hylas! You've been away so *long*! Don't you know I *miss* you?" She turned to Timokles, who stood smiling beside his friend. "Timmi, I think you're *mean*, taking my brother away from me. Why do you *do* such things?"

Timokles said, "It's not my fault, Hermione. He wanted to come. Though I admit, I like to see him. I wish I were coming to Malama with you. Life with Uncle isn't the world's biggest thrill."

"I was only away for a few days, my flower," said Hylas, "and on serious business. I had to see what was happening up here."

"Oh, *serious business*!" Hermione said. "How boring!"

"And I've brought you a present!" Hylas added.

"A present! That makes it better. What is it?"

"It's right here," said Hylas. "Or rather, *she* is. You keep telling me it's time you had a maid of your own. Well, I've bought you one, and here she is."

"Where?"

Eleni had been standing a few feet away while these exchanges were going on, but Hermione hadn't noticed her, any more than she'd noticed the sailors or the workers on the quay. Now, Hylas pointed to her. Hermione's face fell.

"But . . ." she said. "Hylas, you're teasing me. I didn't ask you for a *savage.*"

"She's not a savage," Hylas said. "She's a citizen of the Fortunate Isles, just as you and I and Timmi are."

"Well, she's from one of the out-islands. It's the same thing."

"It's not the same thing at all. Her name's Eleni, and she's a bright, self-respecting girl."

———

"Go on, don't mind me!" said Eleni sourly. "Talk about me as if I weren't here!"

"Her accent!" said Hermione. "I can hardly understand it. All my friends have *proper* maids, from good servant families on Gold Island. You could hardly tell from looking at them that they're not noble. She's positively *swarthy*, and her hair's pitch-black. Hylas, how *could* you?"

Hylas said, "Look at her eyes, my flower."

Reluctantly, Hermione went close to Eleni and looked into her face. Then she said, "Yes, I see. Savages aren't supposed to have blue eyes. But . . . Oh, you are *awful*, Hylas. Everyone will laugh at me. I won't have her, I absolutely won't."

"I just want you to give her a try," Hylas said. "If you haven't taken to her by the time we get to Malama, we'll get rid of her."

"She's dirty," said Hermione. "She smells."

"Well, maybe she does, a bit. She's been sleeping rough and then in the kitchen, and working in the mines. But she'll wash. She won't smell any different from the rest of us when she's been cleaned up a bit. Now, come on, flower, this isn't like you. You're getting an *interesting* servant, not a commonplace one like your friends have. So be yourself, and give the girl a welcome!"

Hylas smiled at his sister with such charm that Eleni didn't see how anyone could resist it. And clearly Hermione couldn't. She wavered, then said, "Oh I suppose I'll have to have her, for now. But I'm telling you, Hylas, once we're back in Malama she'll have to go."

"Then take her to your cabin, or wherever you're going to put her. I'll just have a word with the captain. He'll be wanting to sail while the tide's right. As for you, Eleni, behave yourself and do as you're told, and we'll sort something out in the end. Good luck."

Hermione beckoned to Eleni to follow her up the gangway. Eleni asked, "Where's Andreas?" The assayer said, "He's gone on board already." Eleni said, "All right. In that case, I'm coming."

The ship was spotlessly clean and wholesome-smelling, in contrast to the one that had brought Eleni and Andreas to Orichalcos. Hermione led Eleni to a cabin in the stern, below deck. It was neat but small, with a bunk and a pitcher and basin. In one wall was a closet holding clothes, and in the bottom of the closet was a space.

"That—is—where—you—will—sleep," said Hermione, speaking slowly and distinctly.

Eleni said, "I'm not deaf and I'm not half-witted. You don't have to talk to me in a special voice. I understood everything you were saying to Hylas."

Hermione looked disconcerted. She said, faintly, "He is *Prince* Hylas. Servants refer to him as His Royal Highness."

"All right," Eleni said. "If I'm a servant I'm a servant. I don't mind calling him a royal highness. But I'll still *think* of him as just Hylas."

Hermione recovered her self-possession. "That space is *meant* for a servant," she went on. "There's another cabin like this, next door, where my aunt and her maid are. Aunt Phoebe's supposed to be keeping an eye on me.

You won't see much of her, or the maid either. They were seasick all the way here, and they'll be seasick all the way back."

She put her hands on Eleni's shoulders and looked into her face. "You really *are* a barbarian," she said, "and I never thought I'd be sharing a room with one. But perhaps I'll get used to you. You can't help the color of your hair. If I kept you, I'd have it dyed."

"It's my hair and I don't want it dyed," said Eleni. "Anyway, Hylas said he thought blue eyes and black hair were striking."

" *'Hylas'* again!"

"I mean his royal what-you-said."

"His Royal Highness. Another time remember." Hermione, her head slightly on one side and the tip of her tongue showing between white teeth, studied Eleni for a little longer, then said, "I was wrong about dying your hair. You could be attractive as you are. But you're filthy, and I can't stand that. Go to the galley and tell the cook to send a tub of hot water along."

Eleni found where the ship's galley was and gave the cook Hermione's message. The cook, a stout, greasy Siderian, looked at her with suspicion.

"And who in the Living God's name are *you?*" he inquired.

"I am Princess Hermione's servant," said Eleni with dignity. "Her personal maid."

"Tell me another. A scruffy creature like you!"

"I think it's right," said a seaman. "I saw her come on board."

"And what does our little princess want a tub of hot water for?"

Eleni drew herself up. "You will refer to Princess Hermione as Her Royal Highness," she said.

For a moment the cook was abashed. "I mean Her Royal Highness," he said. But Eleni spoiled the effect she'd produced by going on, "I think she wants it to wash me down."

The cook and the seaman roared with laughter.

"You'll be all the sweeter for it, my duck," the cook said. "Tell her it'll be coming as soon as I can get the water heated. And if she wants any help with the job, she only has to ask."

Eleni returned to the cabin to find Hermione holding up a tunic and cloak, faded and plain but of good material.

"We need clothes for you," she said. "You can't wear things of mine—that wouldn't do at all—but I've borrowed these from Aunt Phoebe's maid. You can change into them when you're clean."

The tub of hot water appeared, dragged into the cabin by the cook and his assistant. The cook made a bob to Hermione, said "Thank you, your Royal Highness," grinned impudently at Eleni, and waddled out. As the door closed, Eleni, on impulse, walked across the cabin imitating his waddle. Hermione giggled. For a moment they were girls together. Then Hermione composed herself and said, "Take those horrible clothes off."

Eleni said, "In front of you?"

"Of course."

"But . . ."

"What are you waiting for? . . . Oh, I see. You were brought up a country girl, and you're modest." Hermione was amused. "How odd. Fancy being ashamed of one's body. I'm rather fond of mine. Go on, Eleni, don't be silly about it."

Eleni was still embarrassed, but felt she'd no alternative. Reluctantly she took off her clothing and stood naked, except for the disc that still hung around her neck. Hermione surveyed her frankly.

"Yes, you're thin," she said. "Thin and flat. Or maybe I should say lean and muscular. Not an ounce of fat. Quite attractive, I'd have thought. But now, what's that thing you're wearing?"

Without asking permission, Hermione drew the medal toward her. She read from it thoughtfully, " 'Who bears me shall see the Living God.' That's quite a promise for a barbarian to carry around with her. Where did you get this thing, Eleni?"

"I was given it," said Eleni.

"Who by?"

"An old woman I met. She found it lying around."

"It's rather nice," Hermione said. "But you're not *really* expecting to see the Living God, are you?"

Eleni, standing naked in front of her interrogator, felt herself at a disadvantage. "Well, now that I've come all this way," she said, "I'd like to. If he exists, that is."

"Oh, he exists all right," Hermione said. "*I* haven't seen him, mind you, except at a distance on Visitation Day. I'm not entitled to. Even Hylas isn't allowed to see the god face to face. My father is, of course, being King. . . ." Her voice trailed away. Then she said, sharply, "We shouldn't be talking about such things. Get in that tub and scrub yourself down. But wash your hair first, while the water's clean."

Eleni got in the tub and began washing, from the top of her head down. Hermione lay on her bunk, watching. "That's better," she said when the water was dirty and Eleni was clean. "Now you're fit to come near civilized people."

As Eleni stepped from the tub, there was a lurch, and she felt movement underfoot.

"We've sailed," Hermione said. "Now, get yourself dry and put on your decent clothes. . . . That's better. You look quite presentable now. Go and tell them in the galley to take the tub away. They can take your old rags, too, and lose them somewhere."

"No, they can't," said Eleni. "I might need them. What if you sack me when we get to Malama?"

"I won't have them around in their present state," Hermione said. "Positively not. And if I did get rid of you, at least I'd send you into the world respectably dressed. But if you have a sentimental attachment to those dreadful things, you can wash them, fold them neatly, and put them where I don't have to see them." She looked with wide harebell eyes into Eleni's deep blue ones. "You're a strange creature, Eleni. I don't think you're a servant at all; I think you're a mystery. And I think I'm going to like you."

———

·XIV·

HERMIONE AND ELENI had their evening meal together in the cabin. This was improper. Hermione should have supped with Aunt Phoebe. The two maids, after waiting on them, should have gone to the galley for their own food and eaten it somewhere out of sight. But Aunt Phoebe's maid, herself green in the face, reported her mistress to be indisposed, and neither of them was seen again. Hermione and Eleni shared a meal that was the most luxurious Eleni had ever eaten: fresh fish, honey bread, a choice of fruit, and watered-and-sweetened wine. Hermione, less impressed than Eleni, said this was all one could expect on board ship.

Hermione could not keep her distance. They were aristocrat and peasant, but they were also two girls of similar age thrown together. From time to time, when she thought of it, Hermione would give Eleni an order or speak to her in a tone of superiority, but she was no more used to having a maid than Eleni was to being one, and the veneer soon wore off. They were intrigued by each other's way of life. Tilling a plot of land, keeping a goat, fishing with the men, seemed as exotic to Hermione as the occupations of ladies in the royal palace at Malama did to Eleni. They talked by lamplight until well into the night.

Eleni, untroubled by the movement of the ship, slept well in her closet and woke at first light. Hermione, on the bunk, was still fast asleep. Eleni looked for some time in wonder at the fair head, petal cheeks, and parted lips, and she admired the slim, pale body that was not much concealed by the shift Hermione slept in. While Eleni had a proper sense of her own worth, and in most ways considered herself as good as anybody else, she couldn't help feeling she was of more common clay. And in talking to Hermione, she'd been deeply aware of her own rough Molybdean accent.

Hermione hadn't asked to be awakened. Eleni went up on deck and found Andreas leaning over the rail on the landward side. He was still wearing the grubby tunic he'd worn all the way from Molybdos, and looked with surprise at Eleni's gown.

"I'm a lady's maid now," she told him. "With Princess Hermione." She couldn't quite keep a note of pride out of her voice.

"I guess I'm still a working lad," said Andreas.

"Myiskus is keeping me busy, sorting out his records."

"We're the lucky ones," Eleni said. "Think of those poor sods in the mines."

"It's not luck really. It's planned."

"So you say," said Eleni skeptically.

They stayed side by side for some time, watching the coast of Gold Island go by. It was a fine autumn day, crisp and clear, and the landscape was a soft, smiling one, with none of Molybdos's ruggedness. Grassed or wooded headlands were interspersed with wide bays; groves of olives or fruit trees with grain fields, cultivated smallholdings, and pasture in endless variety, as if this were land that could do anything it wished. There were scattered farmsteads and white, prosperous-looking villages. The ship moved easily under full sail.

"Have you seen Hylas?" Eleni inquired.

"Prince Hylas? Come with me to the stern!" said Andreas. And Eleni saw that the man working the great steering oar was Hylas himself. As she and Andreas approached, he handed the oar over to a seaman and joined them.

"How's my little sister?" he inquired. "Is she keeping you in order—or is it the other way round?"

Eleni didn't think an answer was called for. She wondered if she should thank Hylas for buying her and Andreas and setting them on their way to Malama. But her mind was full of the sights she'd seen in the orichalc mines, and these in turn had reminded her of the sorry state of her own island. "Listen, Hylas," she said, "you know I come from Molybdos. Well, things are dreadful there, what with the war and all the men going for soldiers and most of them getting killed and the bad weather and the food being seized and everything. When I left, folk there were going hungry. When I came across Sideros, there were people hungry there, too. Then I got to Orichalcos and saw them being driven to death in the mines. And they call these the Fortunate Isles! You're a prince. Can't you do something about it?"

Hylas looked grim. "I'm a prince," he said, "and I sometimes think I can't do anything about anything. I know all about the war. I was in it myself, and got a wound. I shan't forget the men who were killed or got worse wounds than mine. That war changed me completely. It was the lesson of my life. It's still being paid for, in more ways than one. And, Eleni . . ."

Hylas paused for a moment, then went on, "We haven't seen the end of it."

"What do you mean? I thought it was over."

"It's over for the time being. We lost a battle to the mainlanders and pulled our men out—those who were left. But my father's the King, and he hasn't given up. He means to attack again, with a bigger army and fleet. And Theos hates it."

"Who's Theos?" Eleni asked.

"The Living God, to you. We call him Theos, which just means 'God.' My father gave it out that Theos was backing the war. But after we lost, he admitted that it wasn't true. Theos detested it all along."

"Then I'm on Theos's side," Eleni said. "I don't think much of people getting killed or having their legs cut off."

"Nor do I. And I'm not sure that a war can prosper if the Living God won't support it. Priests have argued about that for centuries. But my father won't listen to reason. To tell you the truth, he's crazy for power. He's calling himself Emperor of the Isles and the Western Mainland, and he wants to make that come true before he dies."

"Before he dies? Is he very old, then?"

"Not at all. He's still in his forties. But he thinks he won't live long. He's superstitious, you see. Years ago, some confounded soothsayer told him he'd be killed before he was fifty. Assassinated, by the hand of someone he would never suspect. So he's in a hurry."

"Why should he trouble to be an emperor if he thinks he's going to die?"

"He wants to found a great dynasty." Hylas pulled a face. "He just can't believe it isn't what *I* want. He thinks I'm being awkward at present but I'll come around when the shock of defeat wears off. He expects me to lead the troops into battle again. And although he'd be sorry if I got killed, there'd still be my uncle Leon. Leon's his younger brother, and has two sons. And Leon's loyal; he backs my father all the way."

"But if the Living God doesn't like the war," Eleni said, "can't he stop it? I thought a god could do anything."

Andreas said, "Eleni, I don't think you understand.

The god takes human shape. That's why he's called the Living God. But while he's in human form, he's just like a human."

"You mean he comes under the King?"

Andreas was shocked.

"No, of course not. He's the god. He's holy. No one can touch him, and only the King and the inner priests—the bearers of the Time All One—can talk to him. The life of the Fortunate Isles *depends* on him. You understand? While the god is alive and well in human form on Mount Ayos, the islands are safe."

"So what happens if he gets ill?"

"He changes his human shape. He names another human to take over—it's usually one of the inner priests—and then his spirit changes bodies. The former human shape becomes just an ordinary person, and can be ill or die like anyone else. And the new one becomes the Living God."

Hylas asked. "Do you understand, Eleni?"

"Sort of," said Eleni.

"So you see, the god isn't actually a ruler. It's the King who's the ruler. Mind you, the King isn't supposed to disobey the god directly. He could lose his immortal soul by doing that."

"Then how does the King get around it?"

"By not seeing the god at all. The god's up there on the mountain and my father's below in the city. My father knows that Theos won't approve, so he doesn't see him."

"Seems to me," said Eleni, "that it's time old Theos came down from the mountain and *made* your dad see him."

Hylas pulled a face.

"That's never happened in the history of the Isles," he said. "Once a year the Living God comes down from the mountain, crosses the God's Bridge to the Temple, and shows himself to the people. That's on Visitation Day, which isn't due for months yet. Apart from that, the god stays on Mount Ayos, where he belongs. Some priests say that if he left the mountain, his divinity would lapse. Some even think it'd be the end of the world."

"Take a look at this," said Eleni. She drew out the medal.

Hylas gazed at it, astonished. Eleni told him as much as she'd told Hermione about where it came from.

"I know what it is," Hylas said. "It's the Time All One, and only inner priests should have it. It certainly shouldn't be found lying around. I don't know what to make of you, Eleni. I knew when I first saw you that there was something remarkable about you. But as for seeing Theos . . ."

"It says here I can see him," said Eleni, "and I'm going to. That's what I've gone to all this trouble for. I've got a thing or two to tell this god of yours!"

"This god of *ours*," said Andreas quietly.

Hylas said, "You won't find it easy to get to him, even with the Time All One. But maybe I can help. We'll talk about it in Malama. Meanwhile, here comes Little Sister."

Hermione had arrived on the deck. She embraced Hylas.

"Where were you last night?" she demanded.

"With the captain and Myiskus, of course. It wouldn't do to desert them in favor of the womenfolk. You don't expect the men to talk to *you*, do you?"

"You're teasing me, Hylas. You always tease me. I'm not a child anymore. I expect you were drinking."

"We did put away some wine, I'm afraid. Probably too much."

"Then you were naughty. Don't do it again."

"I shall go back to steering the ship for a while," said Hylas. "Sometimes I think I'd rather have been a seaman than a prince. . . . Have you seen Myiskus this morning?"

"He's up and around," said Hermione, "and saying he has work to do. A dull kind of person, I thought. He wants to know what's happened to his clerk."

"That's me," said Andreas. "I'd better go."

The two girls were left alone.

"I missed you just now," Hermione said plaintively. "Don't you know a lady's maid should be there when her mistress wakes up? To help her dress."

"I shouldn't have thought getting dressed was much of a job," Eleni said.

"You don't understand at *all*," said Hermione. "It's the principle of the thing. You're supposed to be at my beck and call."

Eleni didn't care for being at anyone's beck and call, and her expression must have shown it. Hermione said,

"There, never mind. I'm going back to the cabin. You go to the galley and get some food for us. I'm hungry."

Eleni spent the rest of the day with Hermione, alternately in the cabin and on deck; once again Hermione's efforts to keep a distance were half-hearted and soon faltered. Before the day was over they were on terms of intimacy.

"Shall I tell you something, Eleni?" Hermione said over supper. "Barbarian or not, you're the nearest thing to a friend I've ever had. It's an awful nuisance being royal. You don't have any equals. But somehow *you* don't fit into the picture anywhere. You're so different, rank doesn't really count."

"I expect it counts in Malama," Eleni said.

"It surely does. And we'll be there by dawn tomorrow. I can't say I'm looking forward to it. Once we're on dry land, Aunt Phoebe will be up and about, and everything'll have to be done the way she says, all stiff and starchy. I've enjoyed not having her eye on me all the time, and having somebody my own age for company."

Over the meal, Hermione looked thoughtfully at Eleni several times. When it was cleared away, she said, "Eleni, you're about my size. I think you could wear my gowns. There's one you'd look really good in."

Eleni said, "What would Aunt Phoebe think of *that*?"

Hermione giggled. "She'd be horrified. But she'll never know. Let's try it, just for a little while."

"It's your idea, not mine," said Eleni. "Remember, I'm a barbarian, and a servant, and at your beck and call."

"You sound sour. Don't be like that. And while you're

in my clothes, you won't be any such thing. Of course you won't. You really will be my equal."

"Just for a little while," Eleni said grimly. "And so long as Aunt Phoebe isn't around."

Hermione took no notice. She was already flicking through the gowns in the closet. She pulled out one that was of deep midnight-blue silk, shot through with a vivid kingfisher shade that brightened it as it caught the light.

"Take that servant thing off," she said.

Eleni dropped to the ground the maid's dress that had seemed so splendid the previous day. Hermione pinned the blue gown at her shoulder, then slid onto her upper arm a slender gold armlet. "Now, what about shoes?" she said.

Eleni had never worn shoes. Her feet were too broad for the velvety embroidered slippers that Hermione brought out, but looked elegant enough in a pair of sandals, secured with narrow, thonged ankle straps.

"You have nice slim ankles," Hermione said, "though brown. Stand up. Now turn around. . . . Faster!"

The gown flew out as Eleni twirled around, and the blue silk shone iridescently.

Hermione clapped her hands.

"Marvelous!" she cried. "Oh, if you could see yourself . . ."

There was a tap at the door, and Hylas came in. Hermione stopped short, aghast. She blushed deeply, and stammered, "I w-was just seeing what she looked like. It was curiosity, Hylas. She'll change back in a moment."

Hylas looked hard at Eleni. Eleni had felt exalted,

almost intoxicated. She had seemed to herself as the gown swirled around her to be a creature of another, higher and more beautiful world. Now she stood still, feeling suddenly awkward and unnatural in a garment that didn't belong to her.

Hylas said slowly, "She will not change back. I hope she will never change back. That is how she should be."

Hermione said, "What do you mean, Hylas?"

"Eleni is not a servant. She hasn't the soul of a servant. I can't imagine her being a servant to anyone. Even you."

"But Hylas, you gave her to me. She's mine."

"You must give her back to herself. I'll buy you another maid in Malama. There isn't any shortage of maids. Trained ones, too, that Aunt Phoebe would approve of. But there's only one Eleni."

"I want to keep her," Hermione said.

"There's only one way to keep her. As a friend."

Hermione brightened. "Could I?" she said. "That would be lovely. But would I be allowed? Aunt Phoebe..."

"*I* shall tell Aunt Phoebe about her. When it comes to a pinch, Aunt Phoebe knows her place. I'm the King's son, after all, and the only appeal from me is to my father. And he's so busy planning his war, he hasn't time for anything else. He's not going to care who you bring back with you from a trip."

"Hylas! That's wonderful!" Hermione turned to Eleni. "He gave you to me, and I give you to yourself. Gladly. From this moment you're free. Now come and stay with me in the palace in Malama, as a guest. For as long as we both like. I hope it will be a long time." She giggled.

"I shall say she's a barbarian princess," she told Hylas.

"Me, a princess?" said Eleni. "With my accent? Anyone can tell I come from Molybdos."

"That's where you learned the language, maybe," Hermione said. "I shall invent a history for you. And I shall teach you to speak as we do in Malama."

"I'm not sure I want to," said Eleni, "if it means speaking the fancy way *you* speak."

"Isn't she priceless?" said Hermione. "She's going to be such *fun!*"

Hylas said thoughtfully, "Don't get carried away. We can't really claim she's royal. There are people at court who know all the royals within a month's sailing time. We must rely on something nearer the truth. You're a foundling, Eleni, or so we'd better say."

"*You* found her!" Hermione said to Hylas. "It was clever of you. And how glad I am that you did! Oh, Hylas dear, I'm so grateful!"

·XV·

ELENI WAS AWAKENED soon after dawn the next morning. Hermione was shaking her.

"You must hurry on deck!" she cried. "We're coming into Malama!"

Eleni stumbled bleary-eyed up the companionway behind Hermione. They joined Hylas, Myiskus, and Andreas at the rail on the port side. The sky was clear and already blue overhead, but hazy and pinkish-gold at the horizon. The ship moved slowly and calmly along in a barely perceptible breeze. On their left were first mud flats, then what looked like an army camp, then hundreds and hundreds of low, huddled dwellings, then, finally, a long range of quays at which ships in endless variety of size and height were moored.

They were entering a great harbor. Riding out at anchor were scores of the largest vessels of all: massive high-sided warships with fierce projecting beaks; tall-masted merchantmen with upward-curving bows. Smaller boats plied busily among them; din and clatter and the sounds of raised voices floated over the water.

The ship changed course and headed in toward the city. Eleni and Andreas watched in wonder. Facing them, and curving away on either side into the distance, was a high wall faced with marble—white, black, pink, and green—and crowned with gold spikes.

"The city wall of Malama," Hylas said. "It's a perfect circle, and the royal city's inside it."

Over the wall, domes and towers and airy pinnacles could be glimpsed: some silver, some gold, and some that shone with the reddish fire of orichalc. Outside the city and to the right of the walls rose the mountain—a gentle green at its foot, then purple with heather, then bleakly indigo. From its summit came a tiny glint of gold as something caught the sun.

"Mount Ayos!" Andreas whispered. "The Holy Mountain!" He made the gesture of homage to the Living God; looking around the little party, Eleni saw that the others were making it too. Some impulse she didn't understand caused her to do the same.

Hylas said, "I've seen this sight a score of times before, and it still takes my breath away." Eleni could not say a word.

From the harbor a broad canal led, straight and precise, to a gap in the wall, across which lay a drawbridge. The ship had lowered its sails now, and oars that projected from portholes were moving it along as it nosed into the canal entrance. On the far bank of the canal, outside the wall, were yet more huddled, humble dwellings; as the royal ship was recognized, large numbers of people could be seen flocking to the banks on both sides. They didn't seem any better dressed than those on Molybdos. A shout arose and spread among them, "Hylas! Hylas!"

Hylas, looking embarrassed, waved in acknowledgment.

"You're popular with the plebs these days!" said Myiskus to Hylas, and, to the others, "It's because he's a war hero."

"It isn't that at all," said Hylas. "You're out of touch, friend. Don't you see who they are? Women and children and old folk. They want the men back. They think I have influence, but they don't know how little it is."

The ship moved smartly along the canal toward the drawbridge, which was raised as it approached. Once they were inside the wall, the noise of the crowd was cut off.

Hermione sighed with satisfaction. "Home again!" she said; then, "Welcome, Eleni, to the Golden City. There's nowhere in the world like it!"

Running around the inside of the wall was a ring of parkland with wooded groves, grassy banks, fountains, statues, and winding paths. Where it met the canal was a tiny, toylike harbor, colorful with small boats and surrounded by elegant-looking eating places and pleasure gardens. Then came a ring of water; then another ring of land through which the canal cut its way. Here were fine houses, faced with marble like the city wall and set in spacious green lawns running down to the water.

"The Inner Ring," Hylas told Eleni. "This is where the well-to-do citizens live, and the professionals like Myiskus here. The royals and nobles live in the Citadel."

"And what about ordinary folk? Like me?"

Hermione intervened. She said, frowning, "You must stop thinking of yourself as 'ordinary folk,' Eleni. You're to be one of us, remember?"

"So you say," Eleni muttered.

Hylas said, "Common people don't live inside the walls at all, unless they're servants. Didn't you see the outer city as we came past?"

Eleni recalled the settlement of low, crowded dwellings outside the walls. "I'd rather be on Molybdos than there," she said.

"So would I," Hylas said. "But the city generates a lot of wealth. Some of the poor people go to sea or trade or work inside the walls, and some of them just scavenge. They scrape a living somehow."

Andreas said urgently, "Eleni, look!"

Within the Inner Ring was another circular waterway, which the ship was now crossing. And at the center of this was the four-tiered hub of the city. Fronting on the water were paved squares and immaculately tended formal gardens; behind them an array of splendid palaces, their domes and turrets faced with silver. In the midst of these was a still more magnificent range of buildings that must form the royal palace, faced with orichalc; at the highest, most central point of all was a temple to the Living God, which Eleni and Andreas could recognize at once, for on a pediment above its columns was carved the same motif as on Eleni's medal. From the center of the pediment there soared into the sky a spire that was all of gold. And springing out from the temple—shooting across the land and water zones, clearing the wall to land on the side of Mount Ayos—was a graceful slender bridge, a marvel of construction.

"That's the God's Bridge," said Hylas. "He comes across it once every year, on Visitation Day."

Slowly, in response to shouted orders, the rowers eased the royal ship into its mooring in a little basin separated only by a marble-paved square from the patterned orichalc gatehouse of the royal palace. A gangway was lowered and, in strict order, the royal party disembarked. Hylas went first, then Hermione, then a stout middle-aged lady whom Eleni was seeing for the first time and who was obviously Aunt Phoebe. Myiskus followed, then Andreas and Eleni. Aunt Phoebe's maid and Hylas's manservant stayed on board.

They stood in a little knot on the quay. Hylas looked irritated. Myiskus beckoned to Andreas.

"This is where we remove ourselves," he said. "Come with me to my house on the Inner Ring. We'll find somewhere for you to sleep." He went on, with an edge to his voice, "Remember when in Malama that there's a gap between the ornamental and the useful. Royals are ornamental; you and I are merely useful."

Andreas said, "I want a word with Eleni."

"Be quick, then. And unobtrusive."

Andreas slipped around the back of the group and touched Eleni's arm.

"I'll see you when I can," he whispered. "But don't wait. Get on with it. You *will* see the god, you really will. It's all coming true!"

Eleni didn't answer, but took and pressed his hand for a moment before he went. Then there emerged from the gatehouse a little group of men. They came forward hurriedly. At their head was a tall, soldierly-looking middle-aged man with thinning fair hair and a handsome arrogant face. Next behind him came a gray, elderly man who took Eleni's eye at once, for he wore the garb of a priest, though in finer cloth than she'd seen on a priest before; hanging round his neck, fully displayed, was a disc exactly like the one that lay concealed beneath her gown. Three or four other men followed.

The leader of the group briefly embraced Hylas, then Hermione, then Aunt Phoebe, giving each of them a rapid peck on both cheeks. He didn't give anyone a chance to introduce Eleni.

"I'm sorry, nephew, that we weren't here to welcome you," he said to Hylas, though his tone was not apologetic. "We are in conference with the King, and we must get straight back to it."

"A council of war, Uncle Leon?" inquired Hylas.

"You could call it that, though we are not at war . . . yet."

"And does my father require my presence?"

"He does indeed. He hopes you've come back in a more cooperative mood than when you went. And I must say, Hylas, so do I. Your father didn't take it well that you went off inspecting the mines at a time like this. There are more important matters on his mind."

"He knows what I think," said Hylas. "I don't think it any less. More, in fact. But certainly I'll come. It'll do no harm to tell him again."

"You'll get nowhere if you do," said Leon. "You'll only make him furious. If it were anyone but you, you'd be banished and probably *working* in the mines by now. However, I'm not going to discuss these things out here, and with the women around, too. If you're coming, come."

He turned on his heel and headed back for the gate-house. His entourage followed. Hylas shrugged his shoulders.

"I'm sorry, ladies," he said, "to leave you so rudely, but I think I'd better go. Thank you for your company on the voyage. I hope you settle down comfortably." Eleni fancied his eye was on her as he made this last remark, but she wasn't sure. Then he followed the others.

Aunt Phoebe seemed to have recovered rapidly since setting foot on dry land. She marshaled the little group of women and herded them through the gatehouse and into the royal palace.

Eleni, who'd been dazed by the appearance of Malama, was dazzled afresh by the splendors of the palace. Marble and mosaic were commonplace in its endless rooms and corridors; walls were covered with murals or hung with tapestries; there was furniture finer than she'd ever imagined it could be. Sculpture stood in galleries around courtyards where fountains played. By the time they reached the women's quarters, she had lost her sense of direction.

Aunt Phoebe led the way into a big, airy room, where she and Hermione settled onto couches. Eleni stood uncertainly in the doorway until Aunt Phoebe beckoned her forward.

"So, my dear," Aunt Phoebe said, "you are our newest acquisition. Hylas and Hermione tell me you are to be a friend, not a servant. Well, well. It's not for a mere cousin—for you had better understand that although they are kind enough to call me 'aunt' I am in truth a second cousin—to question their decisions. And indeed, it will be nice for Hermione and me to have some company. Come here and let me look at you."

Eleni went over to her.

"Yes," said Aunt Phoebe, scrutinizing her face, "they are quite right. Blue eyes, and, I think, that indefinable look that distinguishes *us* from the common herd. But the hair . . . I can't agree with them that the effect is so attractive. I'm afraid that to me black hair will always seem plebeian. Hermione dear, don't you think she should have it dyed?"

"Well," said Hermione, "I *did* think so at first. . . ."

"I'm not having it dyed!" said Eleni emphatically.

Aunt Phoebe looked startled. "Really, my dear," she said. "There's no need to speak like that."

"Oh, it's just Eleni's way," Hermione said. "You'll get used to it. She doesn't mean to be rude."

"Eleni. That's a form of Helen, isn't it? Now you're in the palace, wouldn't it be more appropriate . . . ?" But this time Aunt Phoebe intercepted Eleni's look and didn't complete the question.

"Perhaps not," she said. "No doubt you prefer to be dark-haired Eleni. Then I shall accept it with a good grace. I shall think of you as my little barbarian."

Hermione, anticipating further protest from Eleni, said hastily, "She's not a barbarian, she's from Molybdos." But Eleni said, "Oh, that's all right. You can *think* of me any way you like. I don't mind what you think. Don't dye my hair and call me Helen, that's all."

In the next few days Eleni found her place among the ladies. Aunt Phoebe, kindly by nature, quickly grew fond of her and tried hard to suppress her conventional reactions, though she could not help correcting Eleni's pronunciation from time to time. Eleni regarded her accent much as she regarded her name and hair color, and was strongly disposed to stick to it, but she had a tendency to mimicry that betrayed her intentions, and she could sense that her speech was taking on the tones of those around her.

And she felt unbearably confined. Ladies did not move from the women's quarters. They spent long hours in discussion of dress, decoration, manners, meals, and palace gossip; in embroidery, for which Eleni had no enthusiasm; and in playing games with boards, dice, and counters. There were many visitors, all of them aristocratic ladies who joined in these pursuits and in gossip. A favorite subject of conversation was that of Hermione's marriage prospects. The general view was that the King would seek a foreign prince for her and was hoping that after a successful war of conquest he would be able to hook a more important one. Hermione said she wasn't interested in marriage, but no one believed her. There was speculation, which made her blush repeatedly, to the effect that she fancied various young nobles in Malama.

In the evenings entertainers often came in, to play musical instruments, sing, and dance. Hermione had a sweet voice, but could only sing with friends; it would not have done to join in with hired musicians. Eleni, whose voice was a croak, was a disappointment to her in this respect. But Eleni got on well with the visitors, who, like Aunt Phoebe, were fascinated by all she told them about life on Molybdos. None of them had ever before spoken to a plebeian or an out-islander.

In spite of all this ready acceptance, Eleni grew miserable. In the rush of events before arriving in Malama, she hadn't had time to be homesick, but now homesickness came over her in great waves. She longed for her mother and brother, for the streets and quays of Molybdos village and for the hills around it; for rough rural food in place of the palace delicacies. She longed more than anything to be out and about in the open air, but when she suggested a walk in the city, Hermione and Aunt Phoebe were horrified; it was out of the question, they said. She thought of running away; she didn't doubt that she could escape, but that wouldn't help her to complete her quest. What she wanted above all was to do what she had to do and then go home to Molybdos.

Only one outing broke the monotony. On a fine, crisp autumn morning, Hermione suddenly proposed an excursion to the Terraced Garden. Aunt Phoebe, who didn't care for the open air, excused herself; but a palace servant propelled Hermione, Eleni, and three or four of Hermione's friends in a luxuriously cushioned punt through the waterways of Malama to a point on the Outer Ring where a gate in the wall gave access to a small private garden. The young ladies were mildly but pleasurably shocked when Eleni fraternized with the gardeners, and when on the way back she asked for a turn with the punt pole and handled it rather well. Aunt Phoebe had better not hear about these goings-on, they said. Eleni didn't care.

She didn't see anything of Andreas. When she mentioned him to Hermione and Aunt Phoebe, they were gently discouraging. The assayer's clerk was nobody, they pointed out—not suitable company at all for a palace young lady.

Eleni had hoped and expected that Hylas would soon be in touch with her. But the days went by, and she didn't see or hear of him. She felt shy about mentioning his absence to Hermione, and when finally she did so, Hermione looked uneasy.

"To tell you the truth, Eleni," she said, "I believe he's

in trouble with my father. I haven't seen either of them myself. I only know what I've heard at second hand. But I'm told my poor brother's having a hard time. And no, Eleni, you *can't* go looking for him in his quarters, any more than I can. It would be *totally* improper. You'd be turned away."

More than that Hermione couldn't or wouldn't say. The news, or lack of it, increased Eleni's unhappiness. She'd been missing Hylas more than she'd realized, and now she was worried about him as well. But she told herself firmly she couldn't let matters go on drifting. It was up to her to press on with her quest.

She hadn't intended to confide in Hermione, but there didn't seem any other way forward. So the next day she reminded Hermione of the legend on the medal.

"It says I shall see the Living God," she declared, "so I want to see him."

"You'd better speak to the chief city priest first. He's the one who was with Uncle Leon in the reception committee."

"And how do I get to see *him?*"

Hermione said thoughtfully, "For you, it wouldn't be easy. You'd have to get past a lot of underlings. But I'll tell you what, Eleni. I'm a princess of the blood, after all. I'll send a message asking him to call on *me.* Then when he's here, you can talk to him."

The message was sent. Next day there was a reply: the chief city priest was busy but would come when he could. Four more days went by, and he didn't appear.

"I'm afraid that hasn't worked," Hermione said. "I

don't think he means to come." She sounded, if anything, relieved. "It's a matter of power, you see. A woman doesn't have power, even if she's a princess. He won't actually *refuse* my request, but there's no way I can make him carry it out."

Eleni, dejected, went off to walk by herself in the palace's maze of interlocking courtyards and corridors. She'd made an increasing habit of this as she got to know her way around, and she'd hoped that in doing so she would sooner or later encounter Hylas. It had never happened. But today, as she was crossing one of the larger courtyards, a dog ran up and sniffed at her, and she thought she recognized Hylas's hound. Looking up in excitement, she saw his manservant hurrying toward her.

"Miss!" he called. "Miss!"

"You're Dikon, aren't you?"

"Yes, Miss. Prince Hylas's man. The Prince wants to see you, Miss. Needs you urgently, he says. He's fixed it for them to let you in."

"What do you mean, Dikon? Let me in where? What's Hylas doing?"

"He isn't doing anything just now, Miss. He's under arrest."

·XVI·

"UNDER ARREST?" Eleni echoed. "What for?"

"No good asking me, Miss. It was the King's orders, that's all I know."

"Take me to him, Dikon."

"Right you are, Miss. . . . Whirlwind, come here!"

Dikon slipped a lead on the dog, then led Eleni through more passages to a part of the palace she hadn't seen before. He pointed to an archway, through which she could see a small galleried courtyard, open to the air.

"He's in there," he said.

The dog barked excitedly. Dikon patted it on the head. "You can't go to him!" he told it, and led it protesting away. Eleni was left on her own. Approaching the arch, she saw that Hylas was walking in the courtyard, head bent, by himself.

"Hylas!" she called. "Hylas!"

Hylas turned, saw her, and moved toward the arch. Before he could get to where she was, a man in the tunic of a palace guard interposed himself.

"Who are you, lady?" he inquired.

"I'm Eleni from Molybdos."

"Oho." The guard winked broadly. "The Prince's bit of stuff, eh? We know about *you*. Here she is, Highness. All yours."

Eleni was on the point of bursting out with an indignant denial, but as Hylas approached an instinct warned her not to do so. When he greeted her in tender tones and took her in his arms, she didn't resist. A second guard, with insignia that suggested higher rank, came up, smiling.

"I'd go over in the far corner if I were you, Highness," he said. "It's shady there. I can't let you be *really* private, but you can have a bit of kiss-and-cuddle."

"What's all this mean?" Eleni demanded, as she went with Hylas to the other end of the courtyard, three-quarters concealed by a playing fountain from anyone else who might approach. "I'm not your bit of stuff!"

"I'm sorry about that," Hylas said. "It's the only way I can get you in. I'm under arrest, as you can see, confined to this courtyard. But nobody minds if I have a girl with me, under supervision. Helps to keep me quiet, they think."

"But what are you arrested *for*?"

"Opposition to the King. Rebelliousness. Treachery,

you might think from the way my father carries on, though the Living God knows that's not what I intend." Hylas sighed. "My father thought until the other week that I'd change my mind and support him. But now he knows I won't, and he thinks resistance might build up around me. That's why he's had me shut away. I'm lucky he hasn't had me killed, and proclaimed Leon his heir."

"Sounds like things are bad," Eleni said.

"Things are desperate. And moving to a climax, fast. Father and Leon are busy all day long. They're seeing commanders, moneylenders, tax gatherers. There's an army assembling outside the gates, and warships arriving on every tide. Hired mercenaries and rented ships, I may say. The cost's appalling. The orichalc's pouring out in all directions, and we're selling so much it's driving the price down. There's been a fresh tax call on the whole kingdom, and another sweep of the islands to find conscripts. They're bringing in mere lads now. And Eleni, I think you're the last hope!"

"It's up to me, isn't it?" Eleni said. "Me and the Time All One."

"Yes. If you could just get to see Theos . . ."

"That's all right. It says I can see him, and I'm going to. That's what I'm here for. I haven't come all this way to sit in a palace and gossip about who's wearing what clothes and which aristocrat fancies another aristocrat's wife. Now if you'll just tell me how to get up that mountain . . ."

Hylas interrupted her.

"What's happening over there?" he said. And then, "Oh. It's my uncle coming. The daily visit. Listen, Eleni, I may be able to make something work. Whatever I say to Leon, don't object, will you?"

Leon had arrived at the entrance to the courtyard and was exchanging words with the guards. He came over to Hylas with a thin smile on his lips. Uncle and nephew embraced coldly, kissing each other on the cheeks. Leon cast a glance at Eleni.

"I see you are consoling yourself, Hylas," he said. "I wondered why you brought this young lady to the palace, and now it's explained."

"What do you want, Uncle?" Hylas demanded brusquely.

"Your father sent me. He's giving you another chance. He'll still forgive you everything if you'll support him now. You can even have your army command back. So you see how little he *wants* to be at odds with you."

"My dear Leon, he knows that rightly or wrongly, the people out there love me."

"It's not only that, Hylas. *He* loves you. When all's said and done, you're his firstborn and his only legitimate son. The quarrels he's had with you have really grieved him. I'm appealing to you, Hylas; tell him you're sorry and be reconciled."

"No."

"Then you'll stay under restraint, I'm afraid. Unless he decides to do something more drastic with you."

"What, have me killed and put you in my place?"

"It wouldn't be *my* wish, Hylas. I still accept that you're the heir. I hope and expect you'll one day be King, and I shall serve you as loyally as I've served your father. But I strongly disapprove of your attitude. The King is always right, in my opinion, and we should do as he tells us. I wish you'd act accordingly."

"You always were correct, Leon. Thank you. Leave me to think about it. And leave me a little comfort. Let Eleni stay here with me."

Leon's lip curled in distaste.

"We're about to be at war. You're the Crown Prince and the natural war leader. And all you're interested in is having the girl with you. Truly, Hylas, words fail me. But if that's what you want, I'm sure you're welcome to her. I'll tell the guards she can stay as long as she likes."

When he left, Eleni said, "I'm *not* here for your comfort, you know."

Hylas said, "Of course you're not. And has it struck you, Eleni, that our positions are the opposite of what they were a few days ago? You're a lady of the palace now, and I'm a prisoner. I might be put to death. Maybe you shouldn't associate with me."

Eleni said, "Don't talk silly. That's not the way I think."

Hylas said quietly, "Eleni, look at me."

Eleni looked into his eyes, and was startled by the affection in them.

189

"You're . . . fond of me, aren't you?" she said hesitantly.

"I'm very fond of you. Probably more than you can guess. But I don't have designs on you, Eleni. For a very good reason, which I'll tell you when all this is over. If and when."

"We've other things to think about, haven't we?" Eleni said. "What about that mountain?"

"I've been thinking about it for days, Eleni. We've got to get you up there—fast. Now listen: The access to the mountain is guarded, and the guards out there won't let you through. But there's a way to bypass them. Outside the city wall, slanting up toward the mountain, there's the Terraced Garden. A private place, for royals and guests only."

"I know. I've been there."

"Good. Well, you can get into the garden from the city side, and out of it at the back, to a point on the mountain above the guards. The same key opens both front and back doors, and I have one. I've brought it from my quarters; here it is. The back door's hidden behind some bay trees and hardly ever used, so it may be stiff. When you're outside, scramble straight up the mountainside; there's a ceremonial way leading from the God's Bridge at the bottom to the Precinct at the top, but you can't use it because it's lit and patrolled. And when you get up to the Precinct, you must talk the people there into letting you in. That may not be easy. But it's the only chance."

"Andreas said I'd be sure to get there, because it's in the prophecy. But if he was right, I wouldn't even need to *try*. It'd happen anyway."

"I don't think we should count on that."

"Don't worry. I'm not going to. But how do I get out of the palace?"

"Oh, that's not a problem. You haven't been detained. When it gets toward evening, we'll pretend to quarrel and you can walk out on me. That's easy. Until then, please keep me company."

"Oh, *yes!*" said Eleni. "Yes, *please!*"

But as she spoke, the senior of the two guards came striding toward them across the courtyard.

"Miss!" he said. "You're wanted!"

"Who by?"

"The King."

Hylas and Eleni stared at each other.

"What about?" Eleni asked.

"No good asking me, Miss. I just have to take you there."

Eleni said to Hylas, "I shouldn't have thought he knew I existed."

"Maybe Leon mentioned you. But with all this war preparation going on, I wouldn't have thought my father had time. However, you'll have to go, Eleni. He doesn't like to be kept waiting. I'll see you later. I hope. If not . . ."

"If not, I know what to do," Eleni said. "More or less."

Hylas said, "Come here just a moment." He kissed her gently on each cheek. Eleni wondered whether she should kiss him back, asked herself "Why not?," and did. Then she followed the guard through the complex web of courts and corridors.

"This is the King's anteroom," the guard said eventually. "You'll have to wait here till they call you." He left her in a room with mosaic floors and walls covered with paintings of hunting scenes. There were marble benches around it, and a dozen or so men already waiting. Most were blond and blue-eyed, though in a corner was a little group of swarthy dark-haired men wearing fine linen of a kind she'd previously seen only on aristocrats and on Myiskus and the mine managers. No one seemed interested in Eleni. Several of the men were showing signs of impatience, tapping feet or fingers.

Hylas had said that the King didn't like to be kept waiting, but clearly he had no inhibitions about making others wait. Time went by, but no one was called to see him. Eleni grew hungry. A servant came in with a tray of meats and small delicacies, which he offered to the men; he would have passed Eleni by, but she got up crossly and said, "What about me?" Then he allowed her to serve herself.

More time passed. At last a door in the far end of the anteroom opened, and some six or eight men filed out.

"The navy chiefs," said someone on the bench next to Eleni's. "Our turn now, surely."

But after another brief delay, an official appeared in the doorway and called, "The girl from Molybdos!"

Eleni got up and walked between the two rows of men. She could hear dissatisfied mutterings at each side of her. Her heart was thumping; she'd maintained a stolid expression while waiting but it was, after all, rather frightening to be going into the presence of the King himself.

The throne room was large. Eleni had a confused impression of silver and gold and orichalc; of statuary and splendid furnishings. There was indeed a golden throne with a canopy over it, but it was empty. The official motioned her toward a couch on which a man reclined. He had a cup of wine in his hand and was eating from a tray of delicacies similar to those served in the anteroom.

Eleni knew he was the King, though she had vaguely expected him to wear a crown and this man was bareheaded. He was middle-aged, powerfully built and with a formidable presence. He was bald and bullet-headed, and his baldness gave him an almost brutally masculine appearance. He was intent on what he was doing, and not wasting any time over it; he ate rapidly, taking equally rapid swigs from his cup. Finally he licked his fingers and told the attendant to take the tray away and leave the room. He didn't raise his voice, but it was the voice of a man used to instant obedience, and its effect was like that of a whiplash; the servant sprang forward at once to carry out orders.

The King said to Eleni, "Come here. Look at me. Turn round. Face me again. You're a peasant. What are you doing in that gown?"

"Princess Hermione gave it me."

"You're a dark and swarthy peasant from Molybdos. But blue-eyed. Picked up by Hylas and given a gown by Hermione. I want to know more. Are there others on Molybdos with eyes like that?"

"No."

"Who was your father?"

"I don't know."

"Your mother?"

"Anasta. Well, her full name's Anastasia."

"And how old are you?"

"Nearly fifteen."

The King did a rapid calculation on his fingers. Then he said, in the same abrupt tone, without emotion, "You're my daughter."

Eleni stared at him.

"Listen carefully. I shan't say it twice. It was the year I was made an inner priest. My father arranged it. My elder brother was heir to the throne, and my father hoped I would become the Living God next time the spirit moved on. But I jibbed. I didn't want to be a god, or even a priest. Hunting, gaming, and women—that was what I wanted. Father sent me on a trip around the islands to think it over. That was when I met the Molybdos girl. Pretty, in a barbarian way, and loving. I'd forgotten her name, long since, but now that you tell me, I remember it. Anasta."

The King's voice had slowed, but it became brisk again.

"When I left, she knew it was the end. She didn't complain. I didn't know she was pregnant. Maybe she didn't either. Then when I got back to Malama, my brother had died and I was to be King. The priesthood was out. So . . ."

He gave her a fleeting smile.

"You're a child of mine. I have quite a few; don't know exactly how many. Two or three half-castes among them, but not another with your eyes and hair. Interesting. We must have a talk sometime, when I'm not so busy. Just for now, I have to see the money men. Merchants and bankers and other bores."

"When does your war start?" Eleni asked.

"That's not your business, child. Your place is with the women. Run along to their quarters now. I'll see you later. You can kiss me."

He offered a cheek. Eleni, in a state of shock, gave it a brief peck. She received an equally brief kiss in return, and turned to leave. The King called her back.

"I forgot to ask you your name," he said.

"Eleni."

"Eleni. That's all right. I haven't got an Eleni. You can keep it."

"Thank you," Eleni said drily.

As she reached the door, the King called her back again.

———

"Another thing," he said. "Have you slept with Hylas?"

"No," she said.

"Good. Well, don't. Remember, he's your brother."

·XVII·

ELENI WENT OUT THROUGH the anteroom, where the "merchants and bankers and other bores" were still waiting. She had only been a very short time with the King, but it had set her mind in turmoil. She, Eleni, was the King's daughter? She couldn't yet believe it, but she supposed she would come around to doing so; she knew she wouldn't like it.

As for her relationship with Hylas . . . everything was different now. She must go straight to him. It wasn't so easily done as said, for the layout of the palace was complicated, but at length she wound her way to the courtyard where she had left him. It was dusk by now. She had waited in the anteroom a long time.

The guards were still on duty. They let her in at once, and she went to Hylas. He embraced her, gently. Eleni went straight to the point.

"Hylas," she said, "you're my brother. My half-brother. The King said so. When he was on Molybdos, years ago . . ."

"Yes," said Hylas quietly.

Eleni drew back, startled for a second time.

"Hylas! You knew?"

"I didn't know for certain. But I had a pretty good idea. He'd talked from time to time about Molybdos. I knew he'd had some kind of affair there, and the first time I saw you I wondered . . ."

"Why didn't you tell me?"

"Do you really think I should have?"

Eleni considered the matter. Then she said, "No. I'd rather have gone through my life not knowing. But when I came down here, I needed to know. I might have . . . got the wrong idea."

Hylas said, "I knew that once you were here, you'd soon find out. It was best that he should tell you himself. Eleni, I care for you very much, both as a sister and for what you are, but I knew I could never come to you as anything else."

Eleni said, "Maybe I should have guessed." She felt tears coming to her eyes, and told herself sternly that weeping wasn't her way. "It's a lot to get used to," she said, steadying her voice. "I feel as if I've lost you."

Hylas said gently, "Try to feel as if you've *found* me."

"I'll try. It's nice to have you as a brother, I know it is. I can like you that way. But . . . I don't want to be royal, you know. In fact I don't think I can stand it for long.

And"—returning to her normal tones—"you needn't start little-sistering me. I don't take to that kind of thing."

"I wouldn't *dare* to little-sister you," Hylas said, smiling.

"Good. Now I'll get on with the job I'm doing."

"Yes, Eleni," said Hylas. "It's dark now. Time to start. Tomorrow might be too late."

"I'll be on my way, then. What will *you* do?"

"I shall make a temporary peace with my father—tell him I'll reconsider my position. If you do get Theos to come down, I don't want to miss what's going on by being locked up at the time. And if you don't . . . Well, let's not think about that. You're going to succeed."

"I hope," said Eleni. For a moment her spirit quailed. Then determination returned to her. "All right," she said. "I'm off. See you later, brother."

Eleni went back to the women's quarters. From the big room she heard voices raised in conversation. Hermione and Aunt Phoebe had visitors.

"And I'm told she's *with Hylas!*" Hermione was saying. "I can hardly believe it. It's *disastrous* for her reputation. She won't make a good marriage *now*."

"She must be a slyboots," somebody said.

"Oh, I wouldn't say that. Hylas is so handsome. *And* persuasive."

"I hope the poor girl doesn't come to harm," Aunt Phoebe said. "I wish she'd consulted me. I'd have given her some good advice."

———

199

Eleni thought for a moment of bursting in and telling them the truth. But there was no time. She must do what she'd come for. She slipped into the little room that had been allotted to her. There, washed and neatly folded, were the clothes she'd worn on Molybdos and for most of her journey. She took off her gown, changed, and instantly felt more comfortable. The old clothes were practical and unobtrusive; a gown was no good for what she had to do.

She went out—with some apprehension—through the guarded main gate of the palace, but no one challenged her. Going in, she knew, would have been another matter.

In front of the palace gates was a square, marked out with lanterns, and in the darkness beyond it the quay where boats for the palace tied up. Eleni made for the quay. She was wishing with all her heart that she had Andreas with her, as on her earlier adventures. As she was crossing the square, a figure came toward her which she recognized. Myiskus.

She hailed him. He stopped, hesitated for a moment, then said, "Eleni?"

"Yes, it's Eleni. How's Andreas?"

"He's all right. Doing very well."

"You were supposed to let him see me. But he hasn't been to the palace."

"I've needed him all the time. We've been so busy, checking on the orichalc that's flowing out. And now I have to see the King and a clutch of merchants. An urgent summons . . . You can have a word with Andreas now, if you like. I told him to wait for me in the boat."

Myiskus hurried off. Eleni went swiftly to the quay and peered over the edge. There was just one small boat, tied closely to the steps. By the light of a lamp in its bow, she could see a dark head. She called softly, "Andreas!"

"Eleni! It's you!" There was delight in his voice. "I wondered if I'd *ever* get to see you. Hang on. I'll be right up."

"You won't," Eleni said. "I'll be right down. We're going to *need* that boat. Listen!"

Andreas listened. When Eleni had finished, he said, "I'm supposed to be waiting for Myiskus. He'll be furious if he comes out of the palace and his boat's not there. But I don't care, Eleni. This is what we came for."

"Thank the Living God for you!" said Eleni.

"I'm glad you're thanking him for *something*!" Andreas said, casting off. "How do we get to the Terraced Garden?"

Eleni remembered from her previous visit, and told him. The little boat, propelled by Andreas with a single oar, nosed out into the Inner Water. As it did so, an almost-full moon slid out from behind clouds and shone on the marble walls and immaculate gardens of the splendid houses on the Inner Ring. Andreas steered into the canal, along which were several moored vessels. As the boat approached the outer gate, through which the royal ship had entered when they came into Malama, a larger boat than their own, with half a dozen men on board, and carrying a lantern, came toward them.

"The night patrol!" Andreas said. "They want to know everybody's business. Hope they haven't seen us." His lips moved in silent prayer. At the same time he guided the little boat swiftly into the lee of a much larger one. The patrol boat splashed closer, and they heard the sound of voices from it; then it went safely past.

Just before the outer gate, they turned left and wove their way through the small city harbor. The sound of music floated to them now across the water, and soon they were passing on their right a wide, paved and brightly lit quayside area. In its center were fountains, and around its sides were taverns, eating houses and places of entertainment. Blond, beautifully garbed, and aristocratic-looking persons sat on benches outside them. The music came from a trio performing under lanterns in a little low-walled garden. One of the three was playing a flute, another a lyre; the third was singing. The song was familiar to Eleni.

So was the singer.

Eleni couldn't help crying out, "Andreas! Look! It's Nikos!"

The singer was a young man, handsomely robed . . . and blond.

"It can't be Nikos," Andreas said, "with that hair!"

"It is! Look again!"

"Yes, it is," Andreas admitted after a moment. "It really is. So he got away again and came to Malama after all! And dyed himself blond!"

The song ended, amid shouts and waves of approval.

"They think he's good!" Eleni said. "Perhaps he is. I wish we could speak to him. But . . ."

"We can't. Not now."

They went on, past more paved areas, more fountains, more elegant lantern-lit establishments in front of which people sat eating, drinking, talking, or playing what looked like gambling games. Finally the lights and sounds receded, and there were only the quiet grassy slopes and dark glades of the Outer Ring. To the right was the great city wall, with its pale marble facings glimmering faintly through the darkness, and along its top the endless row of gold spikes.

Eleni looked for the tiny landing stage from which, on her previous visit, the royal party had reached the Terraced Garden. She was beginning to think, in panic, that they'd missed it when suddenly it was there, just ahead of them on the right. As the little boat glided up to it, there was the sound of oars from behind, and they were overtaken by the patrol boat. It pulled up alongside, and a voice hailed them: "Who are you?"

Andreas answered, "Andreas from Molybdos. Assayer's assistant to Myiskus."

Somebody said, "Yeah, that's right. Myiskus has a new lad."

The first speaker asked, "Whose boat is it?"

"Myiskus's," said Andreas.

"Do you have permission to be in it?"

"Well . . ."

"Who's that with you? A girl?"

"Yes."

The second speaker said, "Oh, leave 'em alone. They're only young once."

The first said, "All right, kids, we haven't seen you.

203

Have fun. Don't forget to take the boat back." Another man made a noise as of loud kissing. Then the patrol boat pulled away.

Andreas jumped ashore and tied up to a ring on the landing stage. Eleni followed him.

"Wish me luck, Andreas," she said.

"I'm coming with you."

"It isn't worth it. They won't let you into the Precinct. They may not let *me* in. You'd better get back to the palace before you're missed."

"Don't be silly. I'm not dropping out *now*. I know I can't get to see the Living God, but I'll stay with you as long as I can."

Eleni didn't make any further objection. She was thankful to have Andreas's company. She led the way along a tiny winding path through the strip of parkland to where a gate, faced with orichalc and with a crest above it, was set into the city wall. She slid the key that Hylas had given her into the lock. The gate swung open; they slipped through and closed it behind them.

Inside, the garden stood deserted and silent. Moonlight silvered the grass of its lawns. Beyond the lawns the paved terraces rose in steps, one above another. The outer walls of the garden—marbled to match the city walls, and crowned with the same golden spikes—rose with the terraces. High above all loomed the mountain, now very close.

The topmost terrace was planted with shrubs, and Eleni, running up the steps toward it, saw with relief that there was indeed a clump of bay trees. Behind them, more than half hidden, was the little door that Hylas had mentioned. She had to push foliage aside to get to it. The key turned, reluctantly, but the door refused to move. Eleni shoved at it in vain, then backed away to give Andreas a turn. Andreas couldn't shift it either.

"Maybe we could climb over," he said. But looking up at the smooth, high wall and the wicked spikes above, and with no kind of equipment, they could see no hope of that.

"We'll have to try again!" said Eleni. Glancing at Andreas, she saw that his expression was briefly abstracted, and she supposed he was praying. She held back branches to give him as much room as possible. Andreas charged, shoulder forward; the door shuddered but remained shut, and Andreas retreated, rubbing his shoulder. He charged again; it flew open, and he fell through it. He picked himself up and Eleni followed him. They were out on the hillside. The moon, emerging for a moment from cloud, showed them clearly to each other: a scruffy-looking pair in tattered tunics. They laughed and fell forward into one another's arms.

The moon was lost again. They drew apart, and Andreas looked up. "That's a thick bank of cloud it's gone behind," he said. "Just what we need if we're not to be seen. You know, Eleni, the nearer we get, the more certain I am that we're being looked after."

"Save your breath for the climb," said Eleni, closing the Terraced Garden door behind them. She was looking up at the mountainside, steep and dark. She couldn't even see the top.

"Let's have your hand," said Andreas. "Here we go."

It wasn't too hard at first. They could stay upright and even stay hand in hand. Underfoot was sparse grass, then heather, then rough bare soil on which nothing grew. As they got higher, they could see the city below them: ringed with its wall, lit by innumerable lanterns, the shapes of buildings dimly outlined, the palace and temple at the center clearly discernible even though the moon stayed hidden. Springing out from the temple, shooting across the land and water zones, clearing the wall, was the God's Bridge. The mountain end of it was farther around than they were, and now slightly below them. Even from here they could see that it was guarded. Up from it rose the flight of marble steps that formed the ceremonial way to the Precinct. Eleni and Andreas kept the steps at the farthest edge of their field of vision, following a parallel upward course at a safe distance.

As the climb went on, it became harder. They could no longer hold hands, but forced themselves painfully upward on the steepening slope, pausing from time to time to recover their breath and slow their thumping hearts. When they rested, they turned, to see the city even farther below and the outer harbor in view, outlined by lights along the great breakwater. Then everything beneath them grew hazy, the air was damp and chill, and they were in thickening mist. Visibility shrank almost to nothing; the only guide they had to direction was that the right way had to be upward. It seemed that this phase would never end. They plodded on in silence, and Eleni's spirits sank as she climbed. Perhaps this was the end of her; she would die of exposure on the mountainside. Then at last they were out of the mist. The sky had cleared again; there was moonlight, and they could see above them, brightly outlined and darkly shadowed, a wall faced with gold or orichalc that seemed to curve its way around the peak. And the great flight of marble steps was visible again on their left.

They pressed on with renewed energy. But the ground under their feet was growing loose. More and more, they dislodged pebbles from underfoot, until they were barely making headway over scree and volcanic rubble.

"I think we could use the steps now," Andreas said. "They're out of sight from down below." Eleni agreed thankfully, and the last stiff stretch of the climb was up the broad, but still taxing, marble stairway. A gateway faced with the now-familiar orichalc loomed above them and made them feel small and vulnerable. Outside it was a small, narrow, open-fronted booth, and on a little bench in the booth sat a man. He wore the uniform of guards they had seen below in the city.

Andreas, a little ahead and above, turned back toward Eleni and put his fingers to his lips. Then he beckoned her on.

The man was asleep.

They tiptoed past him, through the gateway, and

were in the Precinct. The very top of the mountain was a saucerlike area; it repeated, on a miniature scale and without waterways, the circular pattern of Malama. Its outer ring was paved with marble, and had marble benches dotted around it and many trees and plants in tubs. The next ring seemed to be a single handsome circular building. Raised high in the very center was a great domed temple, identical to the one at the heart of Malama.

The entrance to the circular building faced Eleni and Andreas as they crossed the outer area; they approached it silently and silently entered. They were in a well-lit lobby, from which galleries extended at either side into the shadows. Two men in long white cloaks, one tall and one tubby, were seated on a bench and talking together. They jumped up, startled, as Andreas and Eleni entered. The tall man asked in challenging tones, "Who are you? How did you get in here?"

Andreas, pointing to Eleni, said, "She is the Messenger."

The man said, "What messenger? We don't expect messages this time of night. And you've no business in here. Only priests and lay brothers are allowed in. You're supposed to stay outside with the guard till someone comes to take the message."

Andreas said, "The guard was asleep."

The shorter of the two men said to the first, "He *would* be. They send the worst duds in the whole guard service up here." To Andreas he said, "Well, it must be something urgent if they send you up here at this time of night. What's it about, eh?"

Eleni said impatiently, "This isn't getting us anywhere. Listen, you two: I want to see the Living God."

·XVIII·

THE TWO MEN STARED at her. The tubby one said, in a kindly tone, "Run away home, dear. You can't see the Living God, except on Visitation Day. *Nobody* from outside the Precinct can see him. It isn't allowed."

"Take a look at this," Eleni said. She drew out the medal. The men peered at it. The short one, round-eyed, made the sign of homage to the Living God. The other stared suspiciously at Eleni.

"You needn't ask me where I got it," Eleni told him. "I'm not going to tell you or anyone else. I'm only going to tell *him.*"

The two conferred together in whispers. The tall man said, "Keep them here. I'll go and find Excellency Maronis." He went. Eleni asked, "Who's Excellency Maronis?"

The tubby man said, "He's the Priest-Administrator. The inner priest who runs the precinct. We're only lay brothers. We do what he says."

"Will he take us to the god?"

"I don't know what he'll do. I haven't seen the thing you're wearing anywhere except around an inner priest's neck. He'll have some questions to ask, I wouldn't wonder."

It was some time before the first lay brother reappeared, and when he did he had with him a big, heavy man in late middle age with a high complexion and thinning gray hair. The newcomer, who wore a white cloak trimmed with scarlet, looked irritated.

"*Who* am I supposed to be seeing?" he demanded.

"These two," the lay brother said.

The Priest-Administrator surveyed Eleni and Andreas with distaste. He was obviously not impressed by their youth and clothing. Eleni didn't say anything, but held out the medal, while keeping a grip on it herself. Maronis studied it, told her to turn it over, and said, "It *looks* like a Time All One. Whatever it is, she shouldn't have it."

"Could it be stolen, Excellency?" asked the first lay brother.

"It could be. There are three or four of them unaccounted for. But that's in a period of a thousand years. Most likely it's a fake. But why should someone fake a Time All One and send a scruffy youngster up here with it?"

"It's not a fake," Eleni said.

"We'll look into all this in the morning. In the mean-time, give it to me."

"No," said Eleni.

"What do you mean, 'no'? I'm ordering you."

"And I'm refusing," Eleni said.

Maronis tried to take the medal from her, but Eleni held on tight. "It says I can see the Living God," she said, "and I want to."

"Take it from her," the Priest-Administrator said to the lay brothers. "Then lock both of them up overnight."

The lay brothers looked at Eleni uncertainly. It was obvious there would be resistance, and equally obvious that they were not men of violence. Eleni said, "I'll scream!"

The tubby one said, "Be sensible, dear. Hand it over."

"No."

Reluctantly, the two lay brothers moved toward her. Andreas stepped forward to interpose himself. Eleni screamed, screamed, and screamed again with all the force of her lungs.

The tall lay brother, drawing back, said, "She'll wake *him!*"

Maronis said fiercely, "Stop her, then!"

The tall man put a hand over Eleni's mouth. That didn't prevent Eleni from screaming again, and yet again. The tubby one said, alarmed, "Didn't you hear? You'll wake the Living God!"

Eleni stopped screaming and inquired with interest, "You mean the Living God *sleeps?*"

"When he's in human mode he does. He doesn't when he's in divine mode, naturally."

"And he's in earshot? Good!" Eleni started screaming again. Once again the lay brothers looked reluctant to set hands on her. The Priest-Administrator said disgustedly, "If you can't handle her, one of you go to the gate and fetch the King's guard." And then, a moment afterward, "Too late! Theos is here!" He turned to Eleni and Andreas and rapped out, "Cover your eyes!"

Andreas had put a hand across his eyes already. Eleni left hers uncovered. A man—if man was what he was—came into the lobby. Certainly he looked like a man. He was tall, of medium build, elderly but still vigorous, with a mane of silver hair and a prominent nose. His feet were bare, and he wore a plain white cloak like those of the lay brothers, with no insignia of any kind, but Excellency Maronis and the two lay brothers all made the gesture of homage and dropped a knee. Eleni, without having intended it, did the same.

"I'm sorry about the disturbance, Theos," the inner priest said. "These creatures got into the Precinct somehow, and one of them is in possession of a Time All One, or more likely a fake one. We'll look into it tomorrow."

"It sounded as if someone was being murdered," Theos said. His voice was calm and quiet. "However, I wasn't asleep." He turned to Eleni. "Don't you know your eyes are supposed to be covered?"

"Mine aren't," said Eleni. "I'm the one with the medal. It says I can see the Living God, and if that's you

213

I'm entitled to see you. Not that you look much like a god to me. You look like an ordinary person. A bit better-looking than some, maybe, but that's all."

"A young woman!" said Theos. "And a very outspoken one. I can't remember when I was last spoken to like that."

"I'm sorry," said Maronis again. "We just couldn't deal with her quickly enough. We'll get the Time All One from her, and we'll find out tomorrow where she got it from. You won't be troubled anymore, Theos."

"I am not troubled at all," Theos said. And, to Eleni, "Your observation is quite sound. I do look like an ordinary person. That's because I *am* an ordinary person, until I go into the divine mode. Then I am the Living God; I speak as the Living God and I *know* I am the Living God. But most of the time I am as human as you are. And now, you must show me the Time All One, and tell me how you came by it; and why, since you're not the King or an inner priest, you consider yourself free to come before me uncovered."

"All right," said Eleni, "seeing it's you. I've said all along I'd tell the Living God and nobody else. Andreas, where do I begin? Or will you start? You know all the stuff old Mikele told us. I've forgotten most of it."

Andreas said, in a voice that was awed and a little shaky, "My Lord, she is the Messenger."

"The Messenger?" Theos looked blank at first. Then the mild interest he'd shown was suddenly intensified.

"The Messenger!" he said. "Where do you come from?"

"From Molybdos."

"And who or what sent you?"

"A prophecy, my Lord. The prophecy of Themis."

"Can it really be so?" Theos spoke in an astonished tone. "And this girl, you say, is the Messenger?" He turned to Eleni and said, "Come here. Let me look at you. . . . Yes. You have the eyes and hair. That is the sign. And it may well be time for the prophecy of Themis to be fulfilled. But this is an important, an immensely important matter. I must take a little time to think."

Theos paced the lobby several times by himself, with a remote, absorbed expression. Returning, he looked hard again at Eleni, then at Andreas, whose eyes were still covered. He asked Eleni, "What about this young man? What is he doing here?"

"He's come with me all the way from Molybdos," Eleni said. "I couldn't have got here without him. And whatever happens, I want him with me."

Theos said to Andreas, "Let me see your face."

"My Lord," said Andreas, "I cannot uncover. I do not have the medal and am not an inner priest. It would be sacrilege."

Theos said, "We can't have that. I appoint you, for the time being, a lay brother of the Precinct. Lay brothers can look on me. You hear that, Maronis? He is appointed, here and now."

"Yes, Theos."

"Uncover, Brother Andreas."

Andreas uncovered, and looked into the face of the Living God. His expression was one of such reverence as

Eleni had never seen in her life. He fell to his knees and kissed the hem of Theos's robe.

"All right, that'll do. Now let's get on with it," Theos said briskly. "Let us suppose that this young woman is the Messenger. . . ."

Eleni said, "You're not going to say it can't be me because I'm a girl?"

"Certainly not. On the contrary, the Messenger *must* be a woman. Weren't you aware of that?"

"No."

"That's strange. . . . How did you know of the prophecy?"

"Our priest on Molybdos told us. He saw it in some old scrolls."

"Then perhaps he didn't see all of it. Or the version he read had become corrupted; some stupid male transcriber thought the Messenger could not be female and changed it. Or possibly your priest didn't read to the end. There is more to the prophecy of Themis than that. Much more."

Theos paused a moment. Then he said, "This isn't something to talk about in the lobby. We must go to my cell."

"Your *cell?*" said Eleni, round-eyed.

"My cell. The Precinct is magnificent, as you'll see when you look at it by daylight, but I don't want to live in magnificence. My personal quarters are a little room near this one where cloaks used to be kept. It's very bare. I rise early, eat simply, and think a lot. And I've had plenty to think about lately. These islands are on the way to disaster."

"It's the war, isn't it?" Eleni said. "It's the war that's messed us all up on Molybdos. And, seems to me, if King Whatsit gets it all going again, it'll be the ruin of *everybody*. That's why I'm here."

"You put it very concisely," Theos said. "But before we go further into that, I wonder if you're hungry. I seem to remember that the young have healthy appetites."

Eleni remembered that she hadn't eaten anything since she was in the King's antechamber. That seemed a long time ago, and her stomach suddenly felt hollow.

"I wouldn't mind having a bite to eat," she said. "What about you, Andreas?"

"I haven't eaten all day. Myiskus and I were too busy."

"Bring food to the Living God's room," the Priest-Administrator instructed the lay brothers. Then, holding a lamp, he led the way to a small bare room, only just big enough for four people to sit in comfortably. They were hardly settled when the two lay brothers appeared and laid out a simple meal of bread, cheese, olives, and milk.

"Good night, friends," said Theos, dismissing the lay brothers. "You will remember this night. I believe you've seen the start of something momentous."

With a good deal of help from Andreas, Eleni described what she'd left behind on Molybdos and seen during her journey, including the conditions in the orichalc mines.

"In short," Theos said, "King Basileus is bleeding the

islands dry. He doesn't know, and won't accept, that his campaign against the mainland can't succeed. But it seems that no one can stop him."

"Can't *you*?" Eleni asked.

"He can't defy a direct order from me, on peril of his immortal soul. He knows that. But he thinks I'm safely out of the way up here. The Living God has not descended from Mount Ayos in the past five centuries, other than once a year on Visitation Day."

"However bad you think things are," Eleni said, "they're worse. The King's all ready to go. He might launch his fleet tomorrow. And if he does, there'll be no way of getting it back." She added, "If you're the Living God, you make the rules, don't you? If the King won't come to you, why not go down to him?"

"Even the Living God," said Theos, "doesn't make the rules. The greatest events are all foreordained, though we have not enough prophecies to know what they may be. We have a little light, in the prophecies of Themis and others, but there is vastly more darkness around us. However, Messenger, it is clear to me already that you don't know the whole of the Themis prophecy. You asked, cannot I now go down to the city and confront the King?"

"Yes."

"Messenger, I not only can but *must.* It is so ordained. On the arrival of the Messenger, and not before, the Living God is to descend upon Malama and make known his will to the King."

"Good," said Eleni. "That should cook old Basileus's goose."

Andreas stared at her in mingled awe and horror.

"Eleni!" he said. "How can you take it so *calmly*? Don't you realize? It will be the greatest thing to happen in the Fortunate Isles in five hundred years!"

Theos smiled.

"She's tired," he said to Andreas. "And she's done her duty as Messenger. There'll be more for her to do in another capacity, but I'm not going to trouble her with it now. Maronis and I will organize the Descent while you and she sleep. . . . Do you sleep together?"

Andreas, embarrassed, stammered "W-well . . ."

"Are you lovers?"

"Not exactly. I mean, not completely. But I do love Eleni."

"Don't change the state of things tonight. But to sleep lovingly with another person is good. Maronis shall find you a room where you can have a few hours' peace. You've had a hard day today, and you'll have a harder one tomorrow."

As the two lay down together, Eleni asked, "Is that right, Andreas? Do you love me?"

"Of course I do, Eleni. Didn't you know?"

"Maybe I did. Everything's been so strange, I haven't understood what was going on, and today I got to know something that upset me. But even if things had been as I thought they were and not as they are, I'd have realized in the end."

"Realized what?"

"That I love you too, Andreas. I have all along, really. Ever since we were in Molybdos."

"That's all right, then," said Andreas contentedly. "Now go to sleep."

·XIX·

ELENI SLEPT HAPPILY, aware even through her sleep that Andreas lay warm in her arms. She woke at first light, to see that he was awake already.

"There's a lot of noise and bustle," he said. "We must find out what's going on."

Daylight showed that the room they'd slept in was as rich in orichalc, silver, and marble as the rooms of the palace at Malama. Eleni gave it hardly a glance; she was sated with splendor. She and Andreas went out into the Precinct. Priests and lay brothers milled around busily in the paved area, and there was a general air of excitement. Several of the passersby looked with intense interest at Andreas and Eleni; some even stopped to stare, but no one spoke to them.

They moved, by unspoken consent, to an opening in

the wall that surrounded the Precinct, from which they could look out. The overnight mist had lifted. Directly below them the city of Malama, no larger from here than a cartwheel, was clearly marked out in its pattern of concentric circles. Farther away they could see mountains in one direction and the sea in the other. Early sun shone on a few small slow-moving clouds whose shadows followed them over land or water. As Eleni and Andreas gazed they were joined by Theos.

"The view from my realm," he said. "Or prison, according to how you look at it."

"How long have you been here?" Eleni asked.

"Thirty years ago, the spirit of the Living God moved into me. I didn't expect it. My predecessor took me by surprise when he proclaimed that I was to embody the god. As soon as it was proclaimed, I was filled with the divine spirit, and knew he had spoken truly. I've been in the divine mode many times since then. Everyone in the city was astonished, though. The old King's second son Basileus—the present King—had just become an inner priest, and they all supposed he would become the Living God. It tended to happen to the second sons of kings. But Basileus wasn't suitable, and knew it. The god would have found no home in him. When his older brother died, he became heir to the throne instead, and later it was my duty as Living God to proclaim him King."

"Had *you* been an inner priest?" Andreas asked.

"No. That isn't necessary. The Living God moves into whoever he chooses. I was only a lay brother, and I hadn't been one for long. To tell you the truth, I was on the run. I was a good-for-nothing, violent young man, and wickedly handy with the short knife. I killed another young noble in a tavern brawl, and the best I can say of it is that he was as worthless as I was. I went to Mount Ayos for sanctuary; they took me in and made me a brother. I was full of remorse already. Soon afterward the mortal form of the Living God began to fail. My predecessor, or rather, the god working through my predecessor, decided there was something in me that made me fit to house the Living God's spirit. He proclaimed me, and here I have been ever since. But now it's time for the god to move on again."

"So you'll proclaim a successor?" Andreas said. "How will you choose?"

"*I* don't choose. I am only the mortal shell. Even the god within me, I think, has in the end no choice. What will happen will happen, and when we are in ignorance it is only because we don't have a prophecy to enlighten us. Or perhaps we have the prophecy and don't understand it."

Eleni said, "When the god moves on, the person that he *has* lived in becomes ordinary and will die, same as everybody else; that's what you're saying, isn't it? But will the Living God himself live forever?"

"As long as the islands live. And the islands will live while the Living God lives. But it won't be forever. This mountain is a volcano; the Precinct is built in what was once its crater. It has slept for a thousand years, and in the city they think it is dead. But we have a prophecy. We know it will erupt again and the islands will be destroyed with all their people. We don't know when that will be, but generations to come may wonder if we ever existed."

Eleni felt suddenly dismayed.

"Makes everything we do seem pointless, doesn't it?" she said. "I mean, if the islands are to be blown up and all the folk in them killed, why should we worry what happens now?"

"Nothing goes on forever," Theos said. "What you do today would matter even if you knew you were to die tomorrow. As humans we've only one life and it doesn't last long. All that we possess is what we are and what we do, and we must do what we can."

"I know what *I* want to do," said Eleni. "I've had enough of all this rushing around—all this kinging and godding—to last me a lifetime. I want to get back to Molybdos and live as pleases me. With Andreas."

Theos said gently, "Eleni, you can't. You see, I know what mortal form the Living God will take next."

"That doesn't interest me," Eleni said.

"It does, I'm afraid. I think I told you, there's much more to the prophecy of Themis than you are aware of. For the prophecy tells us . . ." He paused, then went on gravely, ". . . that the Messenger shall become the Living God."

Eleni recoiled, so shocked that her knees went weak and she almost fell. Andreas caught her and held her up. She said, "This is crazy. *You're* crazy."

Theos said, "I am not crazy. I have told you the truth."

"But I'm a girl. Who ever heard of the Living God being a girl?"

"The Living God has no sex. The mortal body the god inhabits has a sex, as it has all other human characteristics. That cannot matter. But, I admit, in human terms it's not a happy fate. The person into whom the god moves must live alone, here on the mountain, with no wife or husband, no child."

"When is this supposed to happen?" Eleni demanded.

"That I can't tell you. It will happen when the god speaks in me. It may be soon and sudden. I told the inner priests this morning that you would be my successor; that's why they're so excited. Some of them don't like it, but they accept it because they must. They have no more choice than you have."

"Listen!" said Eleni. "Me and Andreas are just a pair from Molybdos who've got ourselves tangled up with something we don't understand. All we want is to get the war stopped and go home. *I'm* not a god, and I'm never going to be."

Theos said, "There's no escaping a prophecy. You must prepare yourself, and as swiftly as possible. It is all ordained."

Eleni said, "No, it isn't. I'm getting out of here!"

"You *can't* go," said Andreas. "You won't be able to." And Eleni knew that, for the moment at least, her legs wouldn't carry her. She stood, still in a state of shock, supported by Andreas.

———

Maronis came bustling up.

"Theos!" he said. "We shall be ready soon. The heralds have gone down to the city already, to announce that you're coming. The carriage is being polished up. The Temple priests are robing, those who aren't too ancient to go. The trumpeters are tuning up—a horrible din, they're out of practice, but they'll manage. How long will you be? You've still to robe. And to get into divine mode."

Theos said, "Don't worry, Maronis, there is time." He added, speaking to Eleni and Andreas, "It doesn't take me long to get into divine mode these days. A brief meditation; I open up my mind and the god comes into it. Robing will take longer. And speaking of that, I want you two to be with me in the city. I've appointed you inner priests for the occasion; the other priests know about it already. Maronis, tell the storekeeper they're to be dressed at once for the procession."

"Certainly, Theos," said Maronis. He seemed more harassed than surprised. "Come along, both of you. We must get a move on."

Eleni found herself, with Andreas, hurrying along behind the Priest-Administrator. She had a profound sense of unreality. Everything was out of control, and she was being propelled by something outside her. She said to Andreas, trying hard to convince herself, "When Theos has dealt with the King, we *will* get away from here, won't we?"

Andreas said, "You don't understand, Eleni. What's ordained is ordained. And think of the honor of it, to be the human form of the god!"

"That's not the way it seems to me. Would *you* like to be it?"

Andreas said nothing, but his expression spoke to her. She made a face.

"Yes, you would," she said, answering her own question.

"Eleni, I've said I love you and I mean it. But an honor like *that*, a joy like *that*? I couldn't *not* want it."

"I see," said Eleni glumly. "You'd like to be god. I'd like to be an ordinary girl and have you to sleep with. *That's* the difference. Now I understand."

The lay-brother storekeeper was about to close, on account of the day's events, but he brought out robes of fine white linen, trimmed with scarlet and held in at the waist by scarlet rope belts. Around Eleni's and Andreas's heads he placed circlets of gold, and in the front of each circlet the pattern of the Time All One glowed brightly in orichalc.

"Good thing I keep a few spares," he said; and then, sourly, "You've got quick promotions. I've been here forty years, and still a lay brother!"

Maronis told him sharply to hold his tongue. Then he led Eleni and Andreas to the forecourt of the temple, where some twenty inner priests, similarly robed, were waiting. Maronis took charge and began to marshal the procession. The lay-brother trumpeters, robed in yellow and carrying their instruments, were positioned at the head of it; then came the inner priests in a double file. A space was left, and beyond it were ranged the lay brothers, thirty or forty in number. Then everyone waited. Time went by; the day was advancing, but the air up here was cold. Eleni shivered. At length a lay brother came out of the temple and whispered to Maronis, who announced, "The god has entered mortal form." An expectant hush fell on the gathering, and all who were waiting made the gesture of homage.

Soon afterward four lay-brother bearers emerged, carrying the shafts of a carriage that itself rose above their heads, and over which was a canopy. The sides of the carriage were of silver, with the theme of the Time All One embossed on them in gold and orichalc, and the canopy was fringed with a jeweled gold cloth.

In the carriage—erect, unmoving, and expressionless, so that he might have been an effigy—sat Theos. His robes and headdress were of pure white. He looked straight ahead of him with an austere, expressionless face, as if far removed from the world of ordinary mortals. An aura surrounded him; even the skeptical Eleni felt her spine tingle with a sense of the uncanny. The priests and brothers already in formation turned toward him and, without leaving their positions, once more made the gesture of homage. Theos raised a hand in acknowledgment and dropped it again. But still he gazed unswervingly forward, over all heads.

Andreas, elated, whispered to Eleni, "Now he is the god!"

The carriage moved into position, in the gap left for it. Then, at a signal from Maronis, the procession moved to the head of the great marble staircase that descended the hillside. Maronis himself went first, followed by the trumpeters, their instruments still silent; then came the inner priests; then the carriage, swinging from a frame so that it could stay level on the descent and bearing the rigid, motionless figure of Theos; and, last, the double file of lay brothers.

It was a long descent. The stairway, being shallow, took a winding way down the mountainside. The city was in full view, and had grown larger: the bright curved outline of the walls, the rings of water, the green of gardens and the gilt and marble of great houses; and in the center the high golden gleam of palace and temple. As they moved down, the detail grew clearer and the angle more oblique; the farther walls dropped out of sight and the domes of palace and temple rose to occupy the middle distance. At length the procession approached the God's Bridge. Now the trumpeters raised their instruments to their lips, and the sharp, piercing, almost painful tones went through Eleni's being. This was no martial music, nor indeed did it form anything that her ears could recognize as a tune; it seemed rather to call from a different mode of life beyond her understanding.

The procession broke step to cross the bridge. The gardens of outer and inner rings, the boats on the waterways, were close beneath it now; people were gazing up toward the bridge, and others could be seen hurrying into the citadel. At the inner end of the bridge the square around the temple was crowded with people. They fell back to make way for the procession, which moved steadily forward until it reached the raised central area, surrounded by the pillars that supported the temple roof. In the middle of this central area the King stood. Now he looked like a king, for he was robed in purple and wore a jeweled crown of gold and orichalc. His stance, with feet apart and hands on hips, was upright and arrogant. He waited.

The trumpets fell silent; the trumpeters faded away to the edge of the area. The lay-brother bearers lowered the carriage to the ground. Theos stepped from it, and the bearers in turn retreated. The inner priests formed a half-circle in support of Theos; the King's own entourage made up the other half of the circle. At the center of the circle, the center of the temple, the center of the citadel, the center of the city, God faced King.

Eleni saw that among those closest to the King were Hylas and Leon. But she didn't look long at them; they were not the focus of attention. For it was clear that this was a confrontation. Theos and Basileus looked each other unflinchingly in the eye. Basileus made the gesture of homage; but he did it so perfunctorily, almost mockingly, that it seemed like an insult.

Theos said, "I come as your god, and the people's god." He spoke in tones quite different from those that Eleni and Andreas had heard from him earlier in the morning: tones of a strange resonance that made it sound as if indeed some other power might be speaking through him. The acoustics of the temple magnified his voice so that it rang loud in the ears of all around.

Basileus said, "I bow to the Living God. What is the god's will?" Once again, there was no trace of humility in his voice; he made the words sound like a challenge.

In a steady, still-resonant voice, Theos said, "My will is that you end all preparation for war, disband your army and navy, and send back to their homes all those you have conscripted."

There was a long, long pause. God and King fought a battle of eyes in which neither gave way. Then the King said, loudly, "No!"

Theos said, quietly but with his voice still carrying clearly in the hush that followed, "I am your god, in whom the life of the Fortunate Isles and its people are vested. If you defy me, you imperil your people and your immortal soul."

Basileus said, "I have decided. The war goes on. If it costs me my immortal soul, so be it. I take the responsibility, and the power. I defy you, god. Go back to Mount Ayos and mind your business!"

An awed and audible sigh went around the temple as the King's ringing tones died away. A silence followed. Then Theos said, in a voice at once so quiet and so terrible that Eleni felt fright in the pit of her stomach, "That is your last word, King Basileus?"

"Yes."

"Then it is your last word, King Basileus."

Eleni's eyes could hardly follow what happened next. Swiftly, Theos closed with the King. With his right hand he drew something from beneath his robe. There was a flash of metal. The King's face had just time to record astonishment. Then, with a choked, gasping cry, he keeled over. His limbs twitched; he seemed to try to get up, try to say something that was lost as blood bubbled from his mouth. His head fell back; the fingers of a hand moved; then nothing. Hylas dropped to a knee and bent over him with anguished face. Leon turned in rage on Theos, who had withdrawn the knife and stepped back. Theos drew himself up, and as those around him stared astonished, his air of supernormal authority seemed actually to grow to a climax. Leon stopped short in mid movement, and everyone stayed motionless.

Theos declared, in tones that resounded through the temple, "A murderer became your god; a murderer must cease to be it. The spirit of the Living God now leaves this mortal body, and enters that of Eleni of Molybdos." Eleni, meeting his eyes, was drawn slowly toward him. He fell to his knees before her and said, "I hail you, Thea, the Living God!" His right hand moved swiftly again, the knife jabbed in through his own pure-white robe, and the handle remained protruding from it as the fingers relaxed and Theos himself, with no sound but a brief grunt, fell sideways.

Then the scene unfroze. Panic, confusion, consternation were everywhere. For a moment Eleni felt only the human impulse to help; but she knew that for the King and Theos nothing could be done. Theos had said he was wickedly handy with the short knife; he would have made no mistake. Then came the realization of what had been proclaimed. She felt an exaltation that seemed to sweep her out of her own mind, a sense of being infinitely more than her mere mortal self. For the moment, she believed profoundly. The spirit had moved into her, she was the Living God, she was divine.

She did not make a conscious decision on what to do next. She drew herself up as Theos had done, such a short time before; she felt almost that she was growing, was filling the air around her with her own authority. She heard herself call across the throng, loudly and clearly and in words that seemed to come from outside herself, "I speak as the Living God. Hylas, son of Basileus, I declare you King of the Fortunate Isles! I will wait on the mountain to see you!" Then, the moment she'd spoken, the spirit went out of her as quickly as it had come, and she didn't feel like a god at all. She was the girl from Molybdos, frightened, in a dangerous situation that was far too much for her.

Maronis was close to her, and Andreas was beside him.

"Let's get out of here!" she said. "Fast!"

Maronis was signaling to the chair bearers. Then he and Andreas were helping her into the Living God's throne; the inner priests were streaming away ahead of them. The procession hurried raggedly away from the temple and across the God's Bridge, and began the long ascent. Eleni looked behind, again and again, to see if they were being followed; but there was no pursuit.

Halfway up the great winding stairway, it struck Eleni that she had just seen the violent death of her father.

After the long years of thinking herself fatherless and then the one brief encounter, it was hard to feel a daughter's grief for King Basileus. With his death and the proclamation of Hylas her quest was achieved, for Hylas would surely call off the wars that had brought disaster to Molybdos and all the islands. Yet though she was dry-eyed, there was something within her mortal self that wept bitterly and could find no outlet.

·XX·

"YOU WERE IN DIVINE MODE, down in Malama, Thea," said Maronis as they re-entered the Precinct.

"Yes. I suppose so. It felt funny. Not like me at all."

"You are not in that mode now."

"No," said Eleni. "Now I feel like myself. I feel a bit battered, though. Don't know whether I'm going or coming. I never wanted this job, and I haven't been trained for it."

Maronis smiled. "Nor had your predecessor. He was as surprised as you, and had trouble in learning to open his mind to the god. It takes practice and meditation. But he managed it in the end, and if you remain the god's embodiment for long, you will achieve it too."

"I'm glad you said 'if,'" said Eleni. "I don't want to stay here any longer than I have to. Is there one of your prophecies that throws a bit of light on it? Not that I believe in all that stuff, mind you."

Maronis said, "You are Thea, and it is for you, not me, to interpret the prophecies. You must speak to the Priest-Archivist; he is old and frail, but he knows a great deal. We have a store of scrolls of the highest interest, which you can read for yourself. You will not be short of occupation here."

Eleni made a face.

"I can't read," she said.

Andreas said eagerly, "You'll be able to learn, Eleni—I mean, Thea. Isn't that terrific? You can learn to write, too. And there must be so much knowledge stored here in this Precinct. You might even add to it yourself. And then, to be visited by the Living God in your own flesh . . ." His voice trailed away in wonder and admiration.

Eleni said to Maronis, "I wish I felt as keen as that. Anyway, now I'm here, what do I have to do?"

"You can settle to the life of the Precinct. For you it is a life of meditation. In the immediate future, you can wait for the King."

"You reckon he'll come?"

"Oh, yes, he'll come. You spoke with the voice of the Living God. King Hylas will obey you."

Eleni spent most of the day alone, in silence and in a state of delayed shock. The events down in Malama kept flashing in front of her. She felt deeply guilty: She hadn't wanted the deaths, but it was because of her arrival that they'd happened. She would have felt better if she could have talked to others, especially to Andreas; but it became clear as the day went on that she was not expected to mingle in daily life with the priests and lay brothers. If she was to stay here for long, she decided, she would change that; but the prospect of remaining was one that horrified her. She wondered whether she should meditate and hope to be filled with the spirit of the god; but the thought of it frightened her. She wasn't going to hurry.

Meals were brought to her in a spacious dayroom. She insisted that she would sleep at night in the small bare cell that Theos had occupied, and she retired to it alone. In the night she missed Andreas and yearned for him to come to her. She remembered all too clearly Theos's remark that the person who embodied the Living God could have no wife or husband, no child. And she was sure that Andreas, even if he could get to her room, would never be guilty of so gross an offense as to sleep with the Living God.

In the morning she had an inspiration.

"I want to see the Priest-Archivist," she told Maronis.

A little later an old man with faded blue eyes, sunken cheeks, and a vestige of white hair was brought to the dayroom on the shoulders of two stout lay brothers and deposited in a chair opposite Eleni. He made the gesture of homage and smiled feebly at her.

"It is good of you, Thea," he said, "to find time for me in so brief a godhood as yours."

"A *brief* godhood?" Eleni echoed, her spirits suddenly soaring. "Aren't I going to be it for long, then?"

"If I read the prophecies rightly, you are not. Yours, we are told, will be the briefest embodiment of the god in the islands' history, and will be followed by the longest and most glorious."

"And how's that to happen?"

"That we are not told. If I am right, your successor will be young, but over the years will grow in knowledge and wisdom, and his time will be happy for the islands. I wish I could live to see the start of it, but I haven't long in this world."

"I hope you have long enough," Eleni said.

In midmorning Maronis came to her with the news that Hylas was on his way. They had long warning of the new King's arrival, for he came on foot up the winding stairway, accompanied by Leon, the chief city priest, and two or three counsellors. Eleni insisted that Andreas should join her and Maronis in receiving him. Hylas and his uncle were bareheaded and wore black. Both of them dropped to their knees before her. Hylas said, "I am here, Thea, as you commanded. And I am ready to promise my willing service and obedience."

Eleni felt like herself, not like any divinity, and she spoke in her normal voice.

"You're in mourning, Hylas," she observed.

"Yes, Thea. I am in mourning for my father. I hated what he did, but I loved him as a son."

"And what'll you do now?"

"I think you can guess. The war is off. But it won't be a simple matter, unraveling it all. There'll be the army and navy leaders, the merchants and moneylenders, everyone who was looking for money or glory; it won't please *them*. It doesn't please Leon, either, but he has pledged his support."

"My loyalty is to the Crown, Thea," said Leon, "and Hylas is the rightful King. I cannot do other than support him."

"The soothsayer seems to have got it right," said Hylas, "in telling my father he'd die by the hand of someone he would never suspect. He could hardly have expected to be killed by the Living God."

"Well, it's over now," Eleni said. "And you'll send the men home to Molybdos?"

"To Molybdos and wherever else they came from. It'll be a use for the ships my father hired. I shall close down the orichalc mines as fast as I can."

"And you'll stop seizing crops and so on?"

"Yes. The Fortunate Isles are well named. Given peace, we can support ourselves from our own labor. That's what I want us to do."

"You're going to be busy, Hylas, aren't you?"

"Yes, I am. For as far ahead as I can see. My father kept the reins in his own hands, but I don't like it like that. I want to find a way of running things that doesn't leave it all to me."

Eleni said, "If you've that much to do, I'd better not

———

239

keep you here. You might as well be getting on with it."
She added thoughtfully, "I came from Molybdos to do a
job, and it looks like I've done it. Now I want to get out
of here. How do I do it, Maronis? What's the technique
for telling the god to leave me and go to someone else?"

Maronis, shocked, said, "It isn't up to you in your
mortal form. The god knows what embodiment is suitable
and for how long; and the god will move on when the time
comes. Until then, you are Thea. It is your fate."

Eleni said, "If the god knew how much I want him to
go, he'd do it." As she spoke she felt a sudden swift
premonition that something extraordinary was about to
occur. She looked into Andreas's face and saw that he was
staring at her in astonishment.

"Eleni!" he cried. "Thea! Can't you feel anything
happening? *I* can feel it. I can almost *see* it. You
must . . ."

Then Eleni felt it, as she had in the city the day before.
The Living God was taking possession. She opened her
arms wide. It seemed that with a great rush divinity
flooded into her. She was no longer on the ground, no
longer enclosed in a body; her mind enveloped the Fortunate Isles, the world, and all that was in it. She was the
universe. And she knew it was only for a moment. She
spoke, and her voice came to her, but not through her
hearing and as if it were not her own; it might have been
in the depths of the sea, the heart of the earth, or the
infinitude of the sky. Yet those around her heard it.

"I speak as the Living God," she said. "This is my

mortal form, and I leave it for another. I move to the body of Andreas of Molybdos."

She laid her hands on Andreas's shoulders, and felt the power of the god ebb out of her as swiftly as it had flooded in. As the exaltation left her, she could see it was entering him. His eyes shone so that she could hardly look at him; he had an air that made him seem taller—that made those around him step back involuntarily. Then Hylas and Leon, the chief city priest and Maronis, were all on their knees before him.

Eleni dropped her hands from Andreas's shoulders, but did not follow the others to their knees. She kissed Andreas on the lips.

"*You* believe it," she said. "*You'll* be suitable. *You'll* be happy. Good-bye, Andreas, dear."

She stooped to Hylas.

"You'll do a good job, too," she said. "But I don't belong here. Good-bye, brother. Give my love to my sister. I'm off."

They hardly noticed her. Andreas stood in exaltation; the other two knelt in reverence. With tears pouring down her cheeks, Eleni fled.

·XXI·

ELENI RAN TO HER CELL. She tore off the cloak she'd worn as Thea and removed with it the Time All One. She put on once more the old worn tunic. She raced out of the Precinct and straight down the mountainside, on and on, taking great reckless leaps, almost flying, and miraculously not falling in her headlong rush. The wall of the terraced garden came into sight. Both its doors were unlocked, and she sped through it and across the Outer Ring. The little boat was still tied up. Eleni got into it and rowed swiftly away.

She knew where she was going.

In the quayside tavern where he performed, Nikos was just up from his couch, stretching and yawning.

"Hi, Eleni!" he said. "I heard you were here. Thought you were in the palace, though. What've you been up to? Are you in trouble?"

"Not exactly," said Eleni. "But I want a passage to Molybdos. Help me find one, will you? Quickly."

"You want to go back to Molybdos? You must be crazy. It's great here in Malama. It's *living.*"

"I've had enough of palaces and all that, Niko. It's time I went home."

"Look, why not stay here with me? Be my girl? Have fun?"

"Sorry, Niko, there's nothing doing. Just help me find a ship."

"Well, if you must . . . You've picked the right moment. There's a ship in the outer harbor now that's heading up that way. The skipper'll be in here tonight. I can fix it for you. No problem."

"You'll have to lend me the money."

"Don't worry about it," said Nikos expansively. "I'm making lots of money. *Helions!* And I owe you something for help on the way out. Have the trip on me, Eleni. Give them my love when you get there. Tell them I won't be back."

·XXII·

At dawn, on a dismal gray day of the dying year, a small boat bumped up against the steps of Molybdos quay. Eleni jumped ashore, turning briefly to wave to the sailor who'd dropped her there and who now rowed back to his ship. She wore the torn, shabby tunic in which she'd left Molybdos; she had no money and no possessions.

A man was sitting on a bollard, gazing out to sea. It was Yannis, the headman. He came to meet Eleni as she walked along the quay.

"Morning to you, lad," he said. "You're off the ship out there, aren't you? If you've come from Malama, tell me . . ." He broke off, came closer, then clasped Eleni in his arms.

"It's you!" he said. "Eleni! I didn't know you. You've changed, some way, I don't know how exactly. Maybe

244

you're taller. But where's *he?* My boy, I mean. Andreas. He *was* with you, wasn't he?"

Eleni said, "He's in Malama. He's well, very well."

"But what's he doing there? Why have you come home and not him?"

Eleni was prepared for this question. She didn't think Yannis would believe in Andreas's transformation or even understand it.

"He's in the Precinct, on the Holy Mountain," she said. "In the service of the Living God." That, she thought, was as near to the truth as would make any sense to Yannis.

For a moment Yannis looked grief-stricken. Then he made the gesture of homage.

"It's a high honor," he said, "to serve in the Precinct. Better than being a village priest like old Mikele. It's sad that we won't see him again—they never come down from there, do they?—but a joy that he's alive and doing well. I might have known he'd do us credit. And Nikos? What about *that* young rascal? You know anything about him?"

"Nikos is doing well, too," Eleni said. "He's a performer. They love his singing in Malama. He makes a lot of money. Counts it in helions."

"He always was a performer, if you ask me. And if he's making money, he takes after his dad. Though we can ill spare a strong lad like him, with the men still away."

Eleni said, "The men'll be coming back. That's the news I have for you. The war is off. They'll be home from the army and the mines."

"That's true? Really true? You're sure?"

"I'm sure. I heard it from the lips of Hylas. The old King died and Hylas is King. And Hylas is for peace."

"The Living God be thanked!" said Yannis with feeling.

"I'll go along with that!" said Eleni.

"I thought you were an unbeliever, like your mum. You've changed your mind, Eleni?"

"I don't know," Eleni said. "I just honestly don't know. Seems to me nobody really knows about things like that."

"Well, if the war's off, that's the main thing. We'll get through the winter somehow, and things'll be better in spring. And Dinos still has barrels of wine. We'll have a celebration tonight, for the whole village. For the end of the war, and you being home, and Andreas's honor. Though, to tell you the truth, love, I wish he was home with you!"

With enormous effort, Eleni prevented herself from saying "So do I!" and bursting into tears. Yannis went on, unthinking, "And when the lads are home, I daresay there'll be a husband for you. It'll soon be time for you to be wed."

"I suppose so," said Eleni, without enthusiasm. "In the meantime, what about the boats? Is there still a job for me?"

"There is indeed. Old Klito's been taking the *Seahawk* out every day, and he's a long way past it. He's aching to give up. You can be fishing again tomorrow if you want. And now, I mustn't keep you here. Off you go home to

246

your mum. She doesn't say much, but I reckon she'll be glad to see you."

Smoke was already rising from the cottage when Eleni approached it. Anasta was always up betimes.

"Oh, it's you," she said. "About time you were home. I've missed you, with all the work that needs doing."

"Where's Milos?"

"Gone from here. He got married. A woman whose husband died and left her a holding. They're working it together. She keeps him at it, in spite of his foot, which is more than I could do. Oh well, he's sober, and he helps me two days a week. We manage. I guess it's all for the best."

Anasta bent over the pot.

"I suppose you'll want something to eat," she said.

"I wouldn't mind."

"There's stew in the pot. I can spare a bit."

She put a bowl of stew in front of Eleni and watched her for a while in silence as she ate. Then she asked, "You'll be going back on the fishing?"

"Yes. And I'll learn to heal."

"If Mikele will teach you."

"He will. I can deal with Mikele."

Anasta was silent again. Eleni said, "Aren't you going to ask where I've been and what happened?"

"You can tell me later if you like. Not just now. I've a lot to do."

Eleni took a deep breath.

———

"Mother," she said, "when you were young, were you very beautiful?"

Anasta stared.

"I was better-looking than some," she said. "And a lot of good it did me!"

"It brought you *me*, didn't it?"

"I hope you've not come back here to start on *that* again!" said Anasta crossly. "Anyway, you won't find anything out. I've told you before and I'm telling you now, once for all, you're never going to know!"

"All right," said Eleni. "I won't ask you again." She got up and, on impulse, went to her mother and kissed her on the cheek. Anasta, startled, dabbed at the place with her fingers.

"What's *that* for?" she asked.

"Nothing. I felt like doing it, that's all."

"Well, thank you. Now, if you've finished eating you can make yourself useful. Go and get the goat, and take her up to the pasture."

"I'll go right away," said Eleni.

She set off up the hillside. She was missing her brother Hylas and her sister Hermione; most of all, she was missing Andreas, who might have become her lover and husband. But she was alive and herself, and in her own place. She was Eleni of Molybdos, and she was as happy as could be expected.

The day had brightened. The sky was clear and rainwashed now. Eleni tethered the goat and, turning away from it, raised her eyes to the horizon, to see in the distance the beautiful, frail, enduring image of the Holy Mountain.